SHALLOW WATERS

Center Point
Large Print

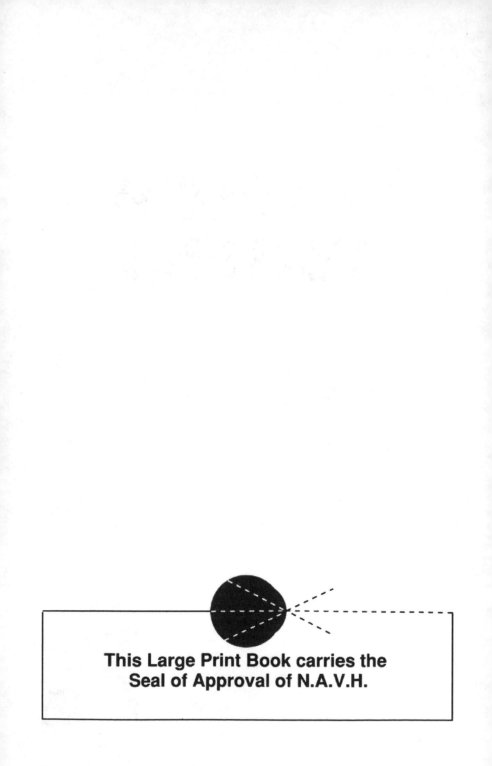

**This Large Print Book carries the
Seal of Approval of N.A.V.H.**

SHALLOW WATERS

A Novel

ANITA KOPACZ

CENTER POINT LARGE PRINT
THORNDIKE, MAINE

*To my mom, dad, and sisters
for putting up with me as a child.
To Sheldon, Sadie, Tela, and Mayan
for putting up with me as
an adult.*

Look at my face—dark as the night—
Yet shining like the sun with love's true light.
I am the black girl who crossed the dark sea
Carrying in my body the seed of the free.

—"The Negro Mother" by Langston Hughes

1526
The transatlantic slave trade begins

Mid-1500s
Stories of Yemaya and Obatala are brought to the New World by enslaved Africans

1807
Britain and the US ban the African slave trade but millions of Africans continue to be traded illegally

1830
The Trail of Tears begins and lasts until 1850

1838
Frederick Douglass escapes slavery in Maryland and becomes an abolitionist, orator, and writer

1841
Ralph Waldo Emerson, an American philosopher and writer, publishes "The Over-Soul"

1848
Richard Dillingham, a Quaker and abolitionist, is arrested in Tennessee for aiding the attempted escape of three enslaved Africans

1849
Harriet "Moses" Tubman escapes slavery in Maryland but will return thirteen times to aid the escape of seventy enslaved Africans via the Underground Railroad

1850
Matilda Joslyn Gage, an abolitionist, author, and women's suffragist, defies the Fugitive Slave Act of 1850, which demands the return of fugitives who ran to free states. She instead shelters them in her home, a stop on the Underground Railroad

1855
Cynthia Hesdra, a wealthy freedwoman, establishes her house in Nyack, New York, as a stop on the Underground Railroad

AUTHOR'S NOTE

As a child, I would stay in the ocean for hours, floating and swimming, submerging myself for impossible lengths of time. My finned tail (acquired upon contact with the salty water) would propel me to fantastical depths. Such are the gifts of childhood.

I would paint the mermaids brown in my coloring books. Though Daryl Hannah and schools of monochromatic mermaids swirled around me, I would draw aside the platinum and golden curtains of their hair to reveal underwater cities full of multihued Black Mer beings! At the time, I had never heard of Yemaya, the Yoruba deity of the sea, who is often depicted as a Black Mer Mother.

Written accounts of Yemaya, originally known as Yemonja, go back as far as the sixteenth century. It is hard to know how old the parables actually are because they have been handed down from generation to generation as oral history in Nigeria. Stories of Yemaya were brought to the New World by enslaved Africans along the Middle Passage. Throughout the African diaspora, from Cuba to Brazil and Haiti to the US, we find different versions of Yemaya. People would hide the fact that they were worshiping her and other Orishas (gods and goddesses) by assigning Catholic saints to each deity. Despite the threat of death, enslaved Africans remained connected to their Orishas and passed on their stories during the most turbulent times.

I wrote *Shallow Waters* to create an empowering narrative with a Black female heroine that takes place during an extremely painful part of American history. Many of us are stepping onto the path of healing our ancestral wounds. The story of Yemaya in *Shallow Waters* is precisely that: a personified tale of my healing. No matter the side of history upon which your ancestors reside, we must all contend with the wounds that are still present today.

Shallow Waters is a mermaid tale (pun intended), both a historical fiction and fantasy. Many of the characters I developed are actual figures from the past. I have shared an accurate timeline because within the novel, some of the events do not occur in chronological order. The rituals and practices that I included throughout the story are a mix of researched facts, experiences, and intuitive recollections.

I hope you enjoy *Shallow Waters*, an offering drawn from the watery depths, a gift from my heart to yours.

FOREWORD

In creating *Shallow Waters*, Anita Kopacz has brilliantly stepped into the role of ritual story-teller, one who borrows the essence of her story from ancient ancestral lore, spins it as a yarn for modern times, and casts it as a soulful summons to the young and the old alike.

A ritual storyteller unleashes a magical power and awakens an inner genius that invites her audience on a mesmerizing journey that captures the heart, releasing it only when the final word of the final sentence has been spoken. Anita has done no less.

Yemaya, the central character, is fashioned from the myth/history of the Yoruba pantheon of gods and goddesses known as Orisha. In the Ifa/Orisha tradition, Yemaya (Yemoja, Yemonja) is respected as the nurturing mother, the Black mermaid who accompanied and watched over the enslaved Africans on their long and treacherous journey from their homeland to the Americas. She is called the Mother of Fishes, fertile life-force energy.

Though Anita demonstrates a keen knowledge of the myth/history, she also clearly knows Yemaya on a personal level. When asked about her connection with the Yemaya energy, she responded, "I would say that my connection is ancestral. My ancestors came from Nigeria and Ghana. My grandmother in St. Kitts would go to the ocean every morning at sunrise and pray. I feel like Yemaya has been with my family line for as long as I can remember."

Shallow Waters is a story of healing and hope, enduring love in the midst of chaos and despair. It is a story that is not only crafted from the realm of the imagination but also released from generational memories held in the DNA. By sharing it, Anita creates space for awakening and releasing the healing energy of Yemaya for today's culture.

Before I met Anita and long before she conceived her story, I researched the Orisha tradition as practiced by African Americans. After many hours of reading and many conversations, I came to an understanding of Yemaya as the name for a Yoruba divinity of the waters, an energy that plays a central role in creating, nurturing, and sustaining life. Etched in my memory is the experience of attending a beautiful ceremony for Yemaya at Rockaway Beach in Queens, New York.

About seventy-five to a hundred devotees, dressed in blue and white, gathered on the shore, bringing watermelons, flowers, and molasses for ritual offerings. They danced to the rhythms of drums, sang their songs and chants of gratitude, and soaked up the vibrant energy of the ocean. A priestess, in an altered state of consciousness, directly channeled the energy of Yemaya and spoke with deep compassion to some of those gathered. She confronted one man about not taking care of his health and sternly invited him to gaze at the ocean and be renewed. Not until I read *Shallow Waters* did I recall this experience. I was a stressed-out doctoral student at the time. Attending the Yemaya ceremony was magnificently refreshing and healing.

The person who invited me to the ceremony was a priestess of Yemaya. When I interviewed her, she explained that she was the mother of six children, that she had always loved children, and that she had always felt a connection to plants and animals, that she talked to them as though they were people. Anita has artfully woven these qualities into the Yemaya of her story.

Just as *Shallow Waters* revived a memory buried in the recesses of my mind, it promises to awaken something in the minds and hearts of its readers . . . some joy, some compassion, some delight, some unknown gift, or some figment of the imagination.

In her story, Anita creates a character who embodies the spirit of the ocean in all of its glory and its power. Driven by the force of an enthralling love, Yemaya follows the ships of the enslaved Africans across the waters and endures many challenges and hardships, all the while displaying her compassionate nature and healing powers.

Perhaps during this present age of a global pandemic, political upheaval, social unrest, and highly charged racial tension, a well-told magical tale, like those of the African griots of the past, can offer a form of cultural healing.

Shallow Waters takes its place among other cultural balms of the twenty-first century, like the screenplay *Black Panther*, coauthored by Ryan Coogler and Joe Robert Cole, and the young adult fantasy novels *Children of Blood and Bone* and its sequel *Children of Virtue and Vengeance*, authored by Tomi Adeyemi. Kopacz, like Coogler, Cole, and Adeyemi, provides space for young people of African descent to see the likes of themselves as heroes and heroines in fantasy tales of superhero magic, mystery, and power. Such stories strengthen one's sense of self and elevate a cultural tradition that has too often been overlooked or misrepresented.

I consider it an honor to have been given the opportunity to pen this foreword. Anita is a dear soul, to whom I am connected in a special way. We are both Geminis and we both deeply loved someone who now resides in the Spirit realm. I knew of her before I met her. My son told me about her free spirit, her radiant smile, her capacity to love and care for her friends, her creative energies, and her nurturing nature. During an impromptu visit to her home in Los Angeles, I experienced all of these qualities. Within minutes, she had ordered food, called friends, and assembled us all around the table for a time of sheer delight, but not without first lighting a candle and inviting the wise and well ancestors to join us. Only she could have written this story, for it comes from within and from beyond, but certainly through the spirit of Yemaya, an incarnate spirit who has traveled with her family for generations.

I hope this riveting tale will captivate you, tickle your fancy, and draw you in as it did me. Maybe it will upset your sleep rhythms and you will find yourself reading it when you thought you would be sleeping. You might find yourself racing through it to see what happens next, thinking you will put it down when you get to the end of the chapter. But let me warn you, that will be very hard to do, for you will be caught in Yemaya's net and you will stay with her until she releases you. You might find your muscles tightening with anticipation or a chuckle escaping your lips. But you will certainly not be bored, and you will most likely be a little bit sad when the story is over. *Shallow Waters* is anything but shallow.

—Velma E. Love, PhD

PROLOGUE

A long grunt escapes my lips. My body is numb. I cough up the last gulp of water I had taken in and held before I passed out. As I sluggishly blink my eyes, one thought repeats in my mind: *I have to break through as soon as possible.* I didn't need to breathe during the transformation, but now my need for air is urgent.

My nerves awaken from the inside out. I can feel the change in my body. Everything is different. My eyes are dry. I blink a few more times in the darkness, working to clear away the crust that has formed over my lashes. Slowly I become aware of a dim light penetrating the shell of my cocoon. The sun's rays reveal a complex webbing within the shell's walls, strong enough to withstand the ocean's waves.

My body stirs, and I can feel the shrunken cocoon chafing against my skin. I pull away from the rough interior. Something's wrong. I'm lying on my back and I can feel that the pod is still—no longer bobbing along the ocean's surface. *I have to get out now!* I push with every molecule of my body, but it's no use. The shell is as hard as rock. I fumble in the darkness trying to find the last section of the cocoon that I had sealed, in hopes that it might be a bit softer. My fingers meet at the top of the pod and I use my thumbnail to puncture a small hole. A bright beam of sunlight streams in and momentarily blinds me. As I had suspected, there is no water. I begin to panic. *Where am I?*

I need the ocean's pressure to help me break through the shell. I frantically chip away at the small hole and attempt to push one of my newly developed legs out. The sensation of being able to move my lower limbs independently throws me off balance. They flail weakly as I try to maneuver them over my body to thrust them up and out.

Although I've watched humans walk and dance and kick, I don't know how to use these new limbs on my own. I grip the backs of my smooth thighs with my hands and pull my knees toward my chest. It's so strange to feel skin and not scales—to have no control over what was once my powerful finned tail. I position my feet against the top of the cocoon and kick the damaged shell with all my strength. The debris shatters away from my body.

Stunned by the bright sunlight again, I clamp my eyes shut and roll over. I strain to push myself up, and wobble as I attempt to stand steady. For the first time in my life, I am vertical, held upright by two feet! I squint through tears and I'm terrified to see that I'm surrounded by a pack of them. Humans who I do not recognize. They don't look like the ones from my home, but I am somewhat relieved to see that they do not look like the pirates, either. I am completely exposed. My body trembles so violently, I'm afraid I will collapse.

1

HIM

Three Months Earlier

The coarse net hits my face and abruptly thrusts me into my bleak reality. I fight with all my might, but it makes no difference. I am ripped from the water. The sting of the crisp morning air shocks me and makes it easy for the fisherman to pull me aboard his splintery boat.

His eyes are the first things I notice. They are deep and dark—like the mysterious realms of the ocean. His hands are gentle and warm, so I surrender to his touch. His coarse hair holds perfect droplets of water as if cradling them until they fall and return to the sea. His skin is so black, I can see a hint of the brilliant blue coral reflected in it. There is something oddly familiar about him.

He lifts the net, gapes at me, and yells something to his friends on the shore. I try to cover my ears because his voice is too loud. Everything is muted in the sea. His deafening tone ignites my will to survive. I begin writhing to free myself, and I manage to flip out of the boat. On the way out, my tail bashes the top edge, and I return to the sea amid the wreckage.

When I look back, he is leaning over the side of his boat. His eyes are alert, and he is breathing heavily. Before he turns back to his companions on the far side of the reef, he spots me. I hold my breath, and I think he does, too. We are frozen in that moment, our eyes glued to each other until his friends come to rescue him. I retreat back to the ocean floor.

His boat returns the next morning, patched with fresh strips of palm wood. I watch as he releases his net into the waters. His strong hands grip the trap, pulling an array of sea life aboard. As he turns to assess his catch, I see the scars on the back of his neck: three straight horizontal slashes.

Obatala!

Ten years have passed since the last time our eyes met. I had erased that day from my memory, but Obatala's scars have reopened deep wounds.

My father knew how much I loved the shells lined with iridescent mother-of-pearl—the shells that could only be found in the shallow waters beyond the reef. I had six of them, one for each year of my life. He'd left early on the morning of my seventh birthday to fetch my gift, promising to be home before our first meal.

We lived in the depths of the sea, in a cave with limited access to the light of day. Mother and I waited until the sun was high above the water. When he didn't return home, my mother decided to go search for him. She made me promise to stay, but as soon as she left, I stealthily followed her into the forbidden waters. Brilliant red coral was scattered throughout the reef, and a school of small yellow fish with black spots darted in and out through the maze. Unlike our home in the cold, dark ocean, the shallows were bathed in sunlight. I caught the flicker of my mother's tail as she dove beyond the ridge. I navigated through the coral to follow her to the other side, where the sea was deeper.

Mother forged forward. The sand beneath us seemed to bubble as we drew closer to land. My eyes darted between my mother and the gurgling seafloor. Something was wrong. Before I had time to warn her, a fog of sand engulfed us. Within seconds, an enormous net dragged me and all the surrounding sea creatures toward the shore. I struggled to find my mother, but it was no use. The coral reef disappeared in the distance.

A human boy around my age dove into the water. As he was examining his catch, our eyes met, and he choked on the seawater. I watched him struggle up to the surface, where he gulped air. But he quickly returned to stare at me. He pulled a small knife from his belt and began to cut through the rope around me. There was still no sign of my mother. The boy finally cut a hole large enough to release me.

I frantically searched the net for my mother

as the animals filed out of the tattered hole. I grabbed on to the twisted rope in desperation. The boy pulled me off just in time to prevent me from being pierced by a long, sharp spear. He urgently motioned for me to flee. A huge man dove into the water to retrieve the spear and patch the hole in the net.

I swam away as fast as I could, far enough to make sure I was safe. When I was a fair distance from the shore, I watched the man scold the young boy. He raised his voice, and I heard him scream the name "Obatala!" The man wrenched Obatala around, pushed him to his knees, and pulled a heavy rope from around his own waist. He hit Obatala across his hands until he cried out in agony. As Obatala's back was toward me, I could see three horizontal scars at the base of his neck. They were raised and discolored and looked like the gills of a shark. Obatala screamed in pain and defiance as he crumpled to the ground. For years after, I heard his wails in my nightmares.

I wanted to save him as he had saved me, but I couldn't rise from the sea to do so. I felt a deep connection with him, like he knew me somehow, in a way no one else ever had. There were lines of fishermen pulling in the net he had rescued me from, so I had to stay out of sight. I cursed my helplessness as my tears mixed with the seawater.

Despite my fear of the shallow waters and the fishermen with their nets and long spears, I returned to that place beyond the reef over and over, hoping to find my parents and to see the boy who'd saved me. It seemed as though he was more like me than any other creature I'd ever known. I could see myself in him. Even though he was a human, he looked like me—the part of me above my fin and scales. He looked like he could have been a part of my family.

A family who I had lost. The six iridescent seashells my father had found for me in the shallow waters are my most precious possessions and at the same time cause me unending pain. When I look at them and hold them in my palms, I feel my parents' souls still with me. They remind me to keep track of each passing birthday, although I'm not sure why I continue to count.

Mother and Father vanished before they could explain to me what I was—not fully human, but also not a sea animal like those we swam alongside in the depths each day. I had never met another creature like us. We were Mer, unlike any other beings we encountered in our days together. My mother would never explain more when I asked about where we came from. She would simply smile and say, "You're special, Yemaya. One day you will know why."

I knew my questions made her uncomfortable, but I wanted to understand why we were so different. I waited years for an answer. But Obatala, finally, is a clue. My fluttering heart tells me so.

• • •

I spy Obatala from my hiding place on the other side of a large jetty. A nearly unbearable yearning makes me want to reach up and gently trace the strong, slightly raised veins on his forearms. I sit in my longing, paralyzed by this new feeling. How could he and I ever be together? His life is completely different from my own. I cannot join him on land, and he could never survive the waters I call home.

Something I cannot fully describe is growing inside me. My heart hurts every time I think about the distance we can never erase. Nonetheless, I return every day to watch him fish, feeling more connected each time.

I often tremble when I first lay eyes on him. He is no longer a boy. He has returned as a man— and has clearly become a leader of his tribe. I see how he is treated with respect and deference. The three scars on the back of his neck have faded, along with the childish curiosity that brought us together once before.

As Obatala releases his net into the ocean, he spots something in the distance and starts yelling. I duck behind a large protruding boulder to keep from being seen. He yells again to a group of friends onshore, much too loudly for me to understand. I don't want to let him out of my sight, but I have to dive into the water for a moment to soothe my ringing ears. Obatala's yelling doesn't penetrate the ocean depths, and though I've learned to decipher the sounds above the water, human screams still overwhelm my senses.

When I surface, I notice beads of sweat forming on Obatala's brow as he frantically rows, collecting his nets from along the reef. He's scared. I see his powerful hands grow unsteady as he pulls up his catch. The source of his terror is invisible from my vantage point. I swim to the far side of the reef for a clear view. Three ships, each larger than a blue whale, approach from the distance. I have never seen such majesty.

Obatala's movements are precise. It's as if his fear has given him mastery as well as speed. There is no longer any hint of the easygoing fisherman he normally is. I follow him, not out of fright but out of curiosity and concern. His muscles flex with the strain of rowing quickly back to shore. I keep my distance.

As Obatala nears the beach, he yells something repeatedly to his village. People rush into their homes and gather everything they can carry. He turns back toward the horizon, and I duck, but he's completely focused on the ships. His boat tips as he stumbles onto the sand and runs into a windswept shack, all the while repeating his urgent warning to anyone within earshot.

The waves are unusually rough, as if a storm is brewing. I dive deeper into the sea and swim into calmer waters. I need to see the ships up close. I surface every once in a while to make sure that I'm on the right course. As I bob above and then beneath the water, I see them. The ships are even larger than I had realized at first glance.

Obatala's single-man rowboat cannot compare to the beauty and power of the three ships in this fleet. As I get closer, I notice something odd. There is a sickly stench of sweat and waste around the ships. I approach the rear of the first one, and a seaman bends over the edge and vomits into the water. Our eyes meet. His salmon-colored face is marbled with burst capillaries. Long yellow tresses matted with oil and dirt cling to his shoulders. The coarse growth on his face reflects the red hue of his skin.

Suddenly, he pulls a wood-and-metal object from his waist and points it at me. A sound blasts through the air—much louder than anything I have ever heard before. I quickly submerge and swim beneath the boat. The blast leaves me unharmed but cuts into a nearby dolphin, who screams underwater as he writhes in pain. I have to hold myself back from catching him in my arms. Nauseated and convulsing with guilt and rage, I am filled with thoughts of revenge. I rush back to shore to see if there is anything I can do to help Obatala escape.

Obatala was absolutely right to be terrified. These strange red men are cruel and fearful beings. What do they want? I cannot stop imagining the horrific things these men are capable of. Water rushes past my ears, creating a constant hum. I have to go and help him! I have to let him know what I've just seen.

I'm not yet comfortable with using my voice, but as I approach the shore, I yell a warning: "Ahhhh!" I try to form the words of Obatala's people, but my vocal cords are not coordinated enough. The scurrying villagers stop and squint in disbelief when they see me, as they strain to trust their vision. I yell again and flip my fin in urgency. The villagers, caught between their curiosity about me and their terror of what they are fleeing, regain their focus and run quickly, farther inland. I yell louder.

Obatala emerges from his palm hut. When he sees me, he runs toward the shore and splashes out into the water.

I continue yelling, trying to form words, desperately attempting to convey the horror of the scene I have just witnessed. As the sea gets deeper, Obatala pulls me into his focus and begins to glide gracefully in my direction. He seems to be aware of nothing but us, ignoring the chaos around him.

Treading water, he gazes steadily into my eyes, and his own well up with tears. Gently, sadly, he caresses my face with his weathered hands. I trace the three scars on the back of his neck, communicating with my touch that I remember his sacrifice. The tragic scene framing our moment of connection recedes. The red-faced men, the horrific stick, and the three approaching ships seem to disappear.

Obatala's face suddenly falls, and he grimaces with fear and regret. He tries to pull away, but it has the opposite effect, as if I'm magnetically drawn closer. I can see that he is resisting the urge to stay by my side, to hold me. Suddenly, he swims away. I reach for him, but he looks toward the ships and commands, "Pirates! Go. Now."

I feel a splash of water hit the side of my face and trickle down the curve of my neck. He splashes me once again and points to the ships in the distance. Obatala floats for a moment more, then turns back to shore. I sink into the water as my heart sinks in my chest. My throat is tight and my stomach cramps as I reluctantly slink out to sea.

A voice inside me calls out: *Wake up!*

Though I want to ignore the message, I know I have made a decision to save my life as well as his. I rise from my numbed state just in time to witness the ships drop anchor. The men Obatala called pirates pile into small boats, and I can see that most of them are armed with more of those deadly staffs. I dive deep and swim farther down the shore.

The scene on land is frantic. The strongest men

30

are ushering the elders, women, and children out of their huts before the approaching boats land. A young boy struggles to untie his baby goat from a tree. He yells out for help. Ignoring him, more of the villagers rush by and head inland. Obatala runs to the boy's side and tries to pull him from the goat. The child tightens his grip. Obatala unsheathes a knife from his belt and cuts the goat free. He motions for the child to follow his clan before he scurries behind a hut.

I feel hopeless once again. I want to scream and wave to distract the pirates, but surely one would finish me off without a thought. I fantasize about exacting revenge alongside my dolphin friends while the cruel men are still on our turf, but I know we would never be able to reach them in time. I keep watch in distress as the small boats reach the shore. A tall, thin, angular man with a hard face sticks a large pole with a colorful flapping cloth into the sand. The pirates erupt from their boats with a loud roar as they rush in waves across the beach.

The village men, women, and children run for their lives. Explosive sounds blast from the pirates' weapons, upsetting the once peaceful sands. Obatala is one of a group of warriors who emerge from their hiding places wielding spears that fly from their hands, but their efforts are useless. They are outnumbered.

"Run!" I plead as I watch the pirates close in

on my fisherman's people. "Run!" Finally, I have found my voice, and the language that I've listened to for years flies from my mouth as I scream.

The able-bodied members of the tribe try to assist the slower ones, but their good deed leads to the capture of the entire village. I am overcome by the sheer terror and hopelessness of the sight.

The pirates force the tribe back to the beach. Fortunately, they no longer seem interested in harming the villagers. I'm relieved when I spot Obatala, until I see him fall to the ground before being dragged by his feet toward the shore. His head dangles lifelessly when the pirates yank him up and attempt to steady him in line with the other villagers. I exhale when I see his face rise once more. White sand cascades down from his woolly cloud of hair and peppers his skin with a thin layer of dust. His arms are held behind his back as the pirates bind his feet and hands together with shiny ropes. Other captives wearing the same cords are lined up behind Obatala, bound to one another and driven ahead. Some weep, and some yell to the gods. Others defy their forced submission by refusing to walk while their captors lead them across the beach. This act of open disobedience earns a strike across the shins from a pirate's smooth leaden branch.

I see a pregnant woman among the villagers, faint from exhaustion and dragged along by her hands and feet. The pirates do not tolerate any captives' attempts to help their fallen companion. In the distance behind this horrifying scene another band of pirates has taken up fire, their torches dancing as they set ransacked huts ablaze.

The villagers fall to their knees upon fully realizing their defeat. The men with the torches return with four horses they've found in the village. The pirates force all of the prisoners back on their feet. The leader, wearing an oversize blue hat the shape of a canoe, paces back and forth in front of the villagers. He stops in front of Obatala.

Two pirates rush over, unchain Obatala, and shove him closer to their captain. He takes a stick and whacks at the insides of Obatala's ankles to spread his legs apart. Obatala's jaw is clenched so hard that the shape of his face is distorted. The leader grabs at it and inspects his every feature, from the backs of his teeth to the undersides of his eyelids. Obatala neither looks away nor fights the man's invasion. The leader violently pushes him back in line, and declares something in his grating tongue.

He begins to pace again, redirecting his attention toward another of the villagers. Handsome, fit, and defiant, the young man looks away. A slight smile crosses the leader's face as he walks up to him. He repeats his inspection with his new victim. The tribesman wrenches back from the man's grasp and spits in his eye.

The leader laughs, wipes the spittle from his face, and snarls.

A group of pirates lumber over to the young man. They release him from bondage and force him front and center. All the while, he kicks and fights. He gets in a few good jabs, but nothing to set him free from their grasp. The young pregnant woman at the end of the line screams, trying to reach out to him, as six pirates lay the young man faceup in the sand with his arms and legs outstretched.

The tribesman calls out for the first time during his ordeal, pleading for protection of the woman and the child within her. I do not think that the pirates understand, but they can see that she is important to him. A pirate takes this cue to rush over, grab her by the hair, and hold her gaze steady toward the young man.

The six pirates tie each of the man's limbs with a separate rope. They arrange four horses around him and fasten the other ends of the ropes to the horses' necks. His wife screams again and tries to break free from the line. The pirate holds on tight but is visibly strained by this tiny woman's strength.

I close my eyes and dive underwater. I already know what is to come next. The beauty of the ocean silence mutes the soul-scorching cries raining down from the beach.

The black feet of the villagers splash into the

water and kick up clouds of sand from the ocean floor. The fog becomes so intense that I am no longer able to see my hand in front of my face. I am forced to swim with my head above water.

The red men get into their rowboats and line up alongside the string of villagers. They unravel strong cords from inside their boats and attach them to the shiny rope that connects the prisoners. When each section is secure, they begin to row forward.

The villagers choke on the salt water as they struggle to stay afloat, paddling as best they can with their restrained legs and feet. The pirates laugh and play a game where they push down on the ropes to submerge the prisoners into the sea. The villagers' struggle to keep air in their lungs as they are whiplashed into and out of the water amuses the pirates to no end.

I can take it no longer. I bash the middle of the last boat with my powerful tail and break the vessel in half. The pirates fall overboard, and just for a moment, a feeling of satisfaction flows through me before I hear them scream.

Within minutes, the pirates reorganize their ranks and continue on their way. Their pace quickens, and they no longer torture the swimming prisoners.

I dive alongside the beautiful stream of black bodies until I reach him. I recognize him from his scars, lingering on the three horizontal lines marking his neck. Obatala ducks underwater as if he has felt me coming. He stares, making no attempt to free himself from bondage. I know what he wants, what he asks without being able to speak.

I mouth, *Yemaya. I'm Yemaya.*

Suddenly he's jerked above water, but I remain by his side until we reach the ships.

He manages to dip below the water one final time, and I hold his hand and squeeze it before they yank him aboard. I don't want to let go, but I can feel his hand being pulled from mine. Just before his fingers slip from my grasp, he's able to return the gesture, and then his hand is gone.

I feel an indescribable emptiness that I know can never be filled by any other. My fate is sealed. He is my destiny. I will follow him. I will find a way to save him.

The villagers are worn as the pirates pull them aboard. Their skin, once glistening and black, is now dull gray and water-wrinkled. Their limp forms waver between a place of life and death.

2

THE MIDDLE PASSAGE

Countless suns rise and fall before I see Obatala again. I'd found a tattered rope attached to the rear of the first ship. At night I tie it around my waist with a special squid knot my father taught me. This allows me a bit of rest. I imagine it's far more pleasant than being held on board.

Sometimes it's hard for me to tell the difference between day and night because the sky seems to get grayer and gloomier the farther away from shore we sail. But today is different. Today the sun is so bright that it warms the surface of the water. As I bathe in this rare pleasure, I see three indistinct faces peer over the edge of the deck. Their gently wavering images are fragmented by what looks like a bit of food landing on the water's surface. Without thinking, I shoot up to snatch the morsel and dive back under the water, where I swallow it whole without chewing. As the ripples fade, I look up again and recognize Obatala standing with two others, a young woman and a little boy.

Obatala's face is gaunt, and he has a scraggly

beard. He looks so much older, so different, so rough. I laugh and gasp at the same time. Against my better judgment, I float to the surface and stare directly at him. I search his face, trying to connect, trying to make eye contact. A slight smile cracks beneath his beard.

I glance at the woman and the boy standing with Obatala, and though they watch me closely, I cannot tell what they're thinking. Their faces are utterly lifeless. Their eyes have sunk into their heads, and their lips are ashen-white and cracked. Bones protrude from their chests. Surely they must need the food they threw in the water for me. I am even more grateful for the flavorless crumbs when I see the sacrifice of their own emaciated bodies.

The farther we go out into the open sea, the more scared I get, and the more I question what I've done. I have no idea where I am, and there is no turning back now—no hope of finding the shallow waters again on my own. But looking into Obatala's eyes for just these few spare moments reminds me that my love for him is greater than any obstacle.

I see the woman whisper to Obatala. Suddenly she is yanked back from the side of the ship. I hear an awful earsplitting shriek as I see an oar swinging through the air. Obatala leans over the side and looks at me with great desperation and fear. A pirate grabs him and pulls him away from the railing. I feel sick, bearing witness to such cruelty with no way to intervene.

I dive deep below the ship to escape from the hopeless situation on deck. The calm of the water provides the solace and retreat I need to survive. Before I can become too lost in the odd beauty of the ocean depths, I return to the ship where Obatala is being kept and fasten myself to it once more with the rope.

The sight of the barnacle-encrusted hull burns its way into my eyes. It reminds me of the beard now growing on Obatala's face. I see his image everywhere. I look out through the murky ocean, beyond the prow of the ship, and I am surrounded by vast stretches of nothingness in every direction. The endless journey is brewing a sort of madness inside me. The sun is beginning to set on this day. The waters around me darken as night falls.

A splash wakes me from my fitful sleep. Something much larger than the food scraps I've grown used to. I untie myself to investigate. I'm repelled by the smell of blood that permeates the water, but I follow its source, knowing that I have to act fast. I spot an object, and as I draw nearer, I see that it is an infant! His eyes are shut tight, and his wrinkly body is sinking slowly. I grab him and push his head above the water. His eyes dart open and stare at me for a moment. Then he coughs as he takes a breath.

I look up and see that the pregnant woman from the beach is slumped over the ship's rail. She does not see her baby or me. She hoists her legs over the side of the ship, and then, as if manipulated by an unseen puppeteer, her arms float wide apart, and she falls gracefully, like a bird gliding in the sky. She hits the surface of the water hard and sinks. She makes no effort to save herself.

I'm momentarily paralyzed with fright. I cannot rescue her while I hold her helpless child in my arms. Suddenly masses of villagers plunge into the water and immediately sink. I can barely hold on to the child as bodies drop into the depths all around me. I hear the pirates yell and hit above us, and even though I know there are atrocities on board, I feel a sense of relief that the terrible men are preventing the rest of the villagers from jumping to deaths of their own.

I hold the baby to my chest, contemplating his awful fate. I'm terrified of the evils that await him on board, but I know I must get him back on the ship, into the hands of someone who will care for him. I watch as the bodies of the villagers grotesquely bob and bounce in the mild ocean waves.

I hear a whisper from above. I look up to see the woman who was with Obatala leaning over the side. She lowers a long rope. I tie it around the baby and kiss him on the forehead.

He is beautiful, a child who should be celebrated with a proper birth ceremony. But bitter is his fate. What will they feed him? His mother's milk lies with her in the salty waters of the sea. I watch with concern as I send him toward a bleak—even if less so than the one that might have been—future. I notice that the woman has a slight spark in her eyes as she lifts the infant over the rail.

Though these fleeting moments sustain me, the journey continues to be arduous. One grim day, as I am swimming a short distance away from the ships to fetch food, I see a cluster of distinctive shapes. Ominously familiar, the sharks are out and circling a large kill. I cannot make out the maimed victim, perhaps a seal or even the dead body of one of the villagers. I have to make my way to the ships before they are diverted from their prey by my presence.

"No fear, no fear," I chant to myself as I swim toward the ships. Any hint of panic and the sharks will home in on me. My tail twitches involuntarily. The great whites can sense my fear and begin their pursuit. My pace quickens. I remember seeing a shiny silver rope dangling from the front of the third ship. Though I am relatively close, the sharks are gaining.

I propel myself out of the water with all the strength I have left. I fly through the air and grab the rope. The momentum of my thrust flings me headfirst into the side of the ship. The impact

41

nearly causes me to lose my grip. The rope is harder than I had imagined, like a bone or rock, and extremely slippery. The water bubbles below. Three shark fins surface and circle.

A pirate yells and points toward the wheel of beasts. I'm hanging under the bow of the ship, so he does not notice me. The men approach the rail, aim their wooden weapons, and blast at the circling threesome, killing the largest one.

I cling to the hard linked rope with an intense will to live. Between the ravenous sharks and the barbaric pirates, my chances of survival are slim. I study the floating carcass in fear that others will arrive once they smell blood. Two men fling a large net into the water and retrieve the dead shark. The pirates rejoice as they begin to haul up their catch.

My fingers are slipping, but I dare not drop into the water. As the waves crash against the hull of the ship, I attempt to compensate for the movement. My knuckles scrape on the weathered wood, and blood slowly seeps from the wounds. My fingers ache, but I welcome the pain because it keeps me focused on what I need to do to stay alive.

My arms shake from holding my weight. I stare into the shark's lifeless eye as it passes near me with the jerky movements of the pirates' net. As soon as they haul the animal on board, I catapult myself off the rope and dive deep into the sea.

I begin to question why I followed these strange vessels. I can barely even muster up the energy to appreciate the boy who once saved me, the boy who now looks more like an old man. An anger within me stews as I think about Obatala. *Why do I love this man? Who is he? Why am I following him? What made me do this?*

My thoughts are so dark that I don't even notice the storm clouds' approach. Lightning strikes the mainmast of the first ship. A brilliant fire breaks out, quickly consuming the sails. Obatala is on that ship! My resentments blow away with the black smoke curling from the canvas. The ship is struck again. The other vessels rush to the rescue, but pirates and captives alike abandon the ship to survive.

There he is! Although his body has deteriorated, his muscles are still powerful as they propel him through the stark chill of the ocean. He is searching for me. I show myself to him, and he swims toward me. His scars seem deeper and more pronounced on his thinning frame.

Our fingertips touch just before he has to return to the surface for air. The chaos around us gives us a moment to connect. He returns to me and gently touches my lips with his fingertips. I don't blink. I don't move. I want this moment to last forever. As he rushes to the surface again to catch his breath, a pirate throws a net over him and begins to haul him up. Our fingers intertwine through the webbing, but neither of us has the strength to fight anymore. We hold on until Obatala is pulled from my grasp and up out of the water, out of my reach once again.

The final leg of the voyage can be compared only to what I've imagined of the last moments before death. I swim less and less. I cannot find the strength to float up for the occasional crumb or small batch of seaweed. The frayed rope I tie myself to every night rubs the scales and flesh from my hips. The few still connected to my tail dance merrily in the water and sunlight, a taunt standing in stark contrast to the all-consuming misery in my heart.

On one endless day, just as my eyes are beginning to droop from weariness, my hip suddenly bumps the rear of the ship. We've stopped! The water around me is shallow. This is new land. *Is this our final destination? What do I do now?* I hadn't conceived of my plan out of water.

My fingers fumble to untie the rope, and I hide behind a large wooden post. Small boats begin the process of unloading the ships' emaciated cargo. The once-proud villagers now barely have the strength to walk on their own two feet. I see Obatala among the group of prisoners being led off the ships and almost don't recognize him. I want to cry out to him and hold his broken body.

But I can't move. Helpless, I watch as he and the other prisoners, all shackled together, shuffle slowly down the gangplank and onto the rough, rocky shore.

I hold back my tears and swim stealthily to a dock, far enough to be out of sight. A memory of my mother flashes across my mind. She is drilling into me the process of becoming human: "We are the only ones left from our Mer village. You need to know every option you have to survive." I listen to the memory as if it were my first time hearing her words. "It will take forty days and forty nights to complete the cocooning process. Make sure you do it somewhere safe, my little dolphin." I can almost feel her cup my face and gently kiss my forehead. She was preparing me for this moment.

A large walkway sits atop dozens of posts that rise above the water's surface. I wrap my tired, injured body around a crusty pillar and use the last morsels of energy within to begin my transformation. Silk fibers emerge from the pores in my back and wrap themselves around me, creating a thin but rock-hard egg-shaped shield around my body.

I now have to eject the water out of the womb I have created. I spin, using my tail for speed. The momentum created expels the remnants through a small hole in the top of the cocoon, which peeks just above the water's surface. When the whirling subsides, I become very still. With the water gone, I cup my hands and gently scrape the protective layer of mucus from my tail and use it to seal the inside walls of the cocoon, making sure to close off the hole at the top.

Just as my mother promised, it does not take long for the thick substance to harden. My vision first blurs, and then I begin to see double. I continue to coat the walls despite my body's desire to shut down. My eyelids finally close. The darkness is absolute.

3

THE AWAKENING

I hear drumming and chanting, and although the rhythm is different from any I've heard at home, the sound is comforting. After breaking through the cocoon, I glance around, hoping to see Obatala's beautiful smiling face. Instead, I look into the strange but inquisitive and kind broad brown faces of the people gathered around me. *Who are these people? Where am I?* The strangers are looking at me almost lovingly, as if I were a newborn baby. Tears begin to well up in my eyes. Not only do I not know where I am, but who I have become is even more of a mystery.

An old woman with straight white hair braided in two long plaits covers my naked body with a soft blanket that feels similar to the downy algae that my mother used. This strange woman embraces me, just as my mother would have. I awkwardly accept her affection, and as I lift my head, the old woman wipes the tears from my eyes. A young girl approaches, and out of an exquisitely beaded bag she wears around her waist she pulls a small carved wooden doll.

She shyly offers it to me. I take it and study the painted designs. Then it occurs to me: the doll is a Mer! The little girl smiles and whispers, "Yemaya." She sits by my side, gazes up at me with sweet expectation, points to herself, and says, "Ozata."

They know me! But how much do they know about me? No one has said my name since my parents died. They have witnessed my metamorphosis. I turn to the old woman. A knowing smile cracks across her shriveled face. I look up and see that the other people who were gathered around me have dispersed. Some are dancing to the drumming, and some have congregated around a fire, laughing and talking. The women are partially covered in brilliantly colored beaded cloth that they wear wrapped around their waists. The men and women both wear bright strands around their necks, wrists, and ankles. They also have elaborate headdresses adorned with beads and feathers. There is jubilation in the air.

In the distance, beyond the dancers, I see structures that are very different from the homes Obatala and his people inhabited. They are tall and pointed, arranged in a semicircle around the edge of a large meadow filled with small yellow and pink flowers. The earth here is different from the white and gray sandy earth at home. This earth is damp, brown, pungent, and dense. I don't smell the ocean. I am nowhere near the place I last saw Obatala.

I am exhausted. The little girl, still by my side, tugs at the blanket that has been wrapped around me. She whispers my name again and gestures toward the dancers, as though encouraging me to join them. The old woman smiles at me, and I understand that I am safe. Something inside me also knows that after I have regained my strength, I will find Obatala again.

The next day, the morning sun peeks through a rip in the tent that housed me for the night. The welcoming arms of this tribe have put my soul at ease in this strange new world. I look around at my small, warm space and see that a fine brown leather covering is laid out for me on the ground. My naked body is wrapped in a soft blanket made of a patchwork of downy fur. I put the leather covering over my body, push my head through the big hole in the top, and stretch my arms through the holes on either side. Still unsure of my new legs, I kneel unsteadily and pull the soft animal skin over me. Smoothing out the wrinkles, I admire the scalloped edge of the bottom of the covering, which reminds me of home and the seashells I used to collect. I am startled by the sound of tiny feet scampering back and forth outside my quarters.

A small brown hand reaches in and sets down a clay bowl with some sort of food in it. Timidly, I reach for the bowl, and the tiny hand disappears as quickly as it appeared. I am alone once again. Still learning to move my long legs, I get them all tangled up as I attempt to grab the bowl and nearly knock it over in the process. I inspect its contents—a curious yellow mush. The color reminds me of the inside of a sea urchin, but the texture is rough. I scoop the food up with my fingers and revel in the experience of eating in my new form. Mer never use their noses to smell, and I realize now how it heightens the flavor of the food. Before my transformation, my nose seemed like a useless thing, but now I am in awe of its ability.

I gulp down the last of the food. The little girl's tiny hand reaches in again and grabs the empty bowl. Without thinking I leap up to follow her. I trip over my legs and almost land facedown more than once, but I am able to gain control enough to propel myself out of the tent. The young girl, Ozata, is running with the empty bowl in her hands through the center of the semicircle of tents. I am right behind her when she stops for a moment in front of a structure that is much larger than the tent I slept in. Her long black braids sway from side to side as she disappears into the folds of a painted canopy covering the opening.

I see the elder woman standing off to the side of the large, rounded tent. She walks over to me and unexpectedly engulfs me in her delicate yet deceptively strong arms. She steadies me on my feet, reassuring me with a warm hug. Then, with extreme patience, she ushers me toward the tent opening and lifts the painted flap to reveal the dark entrance. Trails of scented smoke drift through the slit, momentarily obscuring my vision. Her gentle hands guide me into the middle of the whale-shaped structure as my vision slowly adjusts to the dim light within. I look around and notice the mighty wooden rods that hold the giant tent together.

The woman motions for me to sit in the center of an animal-skin rug. I can feel its coarse yet comforting fur on the backs of my newly formed thighs. A younger woman emerges from the shadows and sits to my right, while the elder woman settles down on my left. They begin to recite words in a foreign tongue. After listening for a few minutes, I realize they are speaking two different languages.

The elder woman turns to me and says, "Yemaya, I am speaking the language of my people. I am Cora, and this is my daughter, Amitola."

Amitola nods and begins to speak to me in the other language. "I speak to you in the tongue of the white man."

I freeze and stare at her, hearing the harsh tones of the pirates echo in my ears.

Amitola continues, "The white man has taken

over the land. Many of the elders have refused to speak their language, but in order for our people to survive, it is vital for us to understand what they are saying."

"I choose to speak the tongue of your people," I conclude.

Ozata runs in and jumps on Amitola's lap. "Mama!"

Amitola caresses Ozata's back and continues to speak.

"We must imbue you with the knowledge of both languages for your safety and survival."

I consider her words carefully. I know that she is right, so I concentrate on the language, listening deeply, taking in the new words and phrases quickly as I bend their sounds and grammar to my own.

Amitola whispers something in Ozata's ears as she squeezes her once more. Ozata giggles, shimmies out of her mother's arms, and runs to the flap in the tent. A brief stream of sunlight captures her silhouette as she rushes out.

"We consulted with the council to see your fate," Cora says as she motions for a man, who has been standing in the corner, to come closer to us. As he approaches, I realize that he is dressed in the same garb as the village women.

"They told us who you were and how to teach you the language of this land. You have the capacity to learn much faster than humans. We will be blessed by your presence for only a few days." Cora speaks these words with no emotion. She continues, "Although you will get what you came for, there are many other things that color your path. The road will be long and hard."

Cora motions for the man to stand behind me. He is wearing a long leather dress with red and yellow beads crawling in intricate designs up his sleeves. He smells sweet, like he has soaked in flowers. I inhale deeply as he places his hands gently on my shoulders.

"Now it is time for your medicine animal to contact you."

I'm confused but I do not interrupt Cora. She says that my medicine animal will help me understand my journey. It will give me clues along my path. She explains that everyone in the tribe has one, even Ozata. Cora hands me a small wooden cup filled with a pungent liquid.

Shivering with fear and anticipation, I choke down the liquid and ask, "What is my fate?"

"We know why you are here on our land. It is not by chance that you were delivered into our hands, and we are meant to assist you on your journey. But you must discover your own fate for yourself. The medicine will help you see clearly."

Cora picks up a small bundle that looks like dried weeds wrapped securely in field grass. She ignites the tip of the bundle in the fire. She removes it and then extinguishes the flames, but the end continues to glow and emit a heady, thick, musty sweet smoke. She hands the bundle to the man standing behind me and he waves the smoking weeds over my head and around my body. I am mesmerized by the glowing embers and intoxicated by the smoke. I sneeze as he chants something I do not understand. He places the bundle in a seashell, much like the ones my father would fetch me, and then taps me three times gently but firmly between my eyebrows. I feel stunned, then fall deep within myself.

My eyes roll to the back of my head, and my body becomes weightless as I awaken in a dream state. Ahead of me, a clear river swims through the forest, bathing lush vegetation in the shimmering reflection of the midday sun. There is no sign of humankind here. The tickle of damp grass teases my toes. I look down at my bare feet as I massage them into the moist earth.

A stick snaps in the distance. I focus my attention on the noise. As I squint to sharpen my vision, I see Obatala. He notices and casually rubs the back of his neck. I begin to move toward him, but he turns away from me and runs. His pace is slow, as if he knows I will follow. I swipe at low-hanging branches and overgrown weeds as I chase him. I get close enough to see the three scars on the back of his neck. He stops, and we almost collide.

I reach out and trace the scars with my fingers. My body begins to tingle, but before I can whisper his name, a deafening roar almost knocks me to the ground. I jerk my head around, but nothing is there. When I look back at Obatala, he's gone.

I hear the roar again. I blame the animal for scaring away Obatala. My anger abates any fear of the approaching brute. I am steady. My feet are anchored in the soil. The mighty beast's breath is on my cheek. She is but a fraction of an inch away from my face. Her eyes, black as midnight, stare into my own. Then I hear the faint sound of drums. The steady rhythm calms my anger. The drums crescendo as the beat quickens.

I have no fear. Her presence does not threaten me. I stare at her—a black panther, waiting for my message. I notice my reflection staring back at me in her eyes. My mirror image slowly morphs, though I am standing completely still. I see myself running on my new legs; I see the white men attacking Cora and her tribe.

The panther blinks. Before I can fully understand what I've seen, she turns and runs away. I close my eyes and awaken to my life. I feel my legs. There are fresh scrapes and bruises from the forest underbrush in my dream.

Before I am fully alert, I call for Cora, though she has never left my side. She calms me by placing her hand on my shoulder and whispering in her native tongue, "Hush, my child; you must not speak about anything that you saw."

"But I have to! You're in—"

"No! The ancestors told me I must not listen to your vision."

My eyes flash with pain, but I hold my tongue.

"Why would the panther show me what's going to happen if I'm not supposed to warn you?" I cry as I recall the horrible scene I saw of her tribe being captured.

Cora remains composed and says, "The wind has brought the message from the south. Our spirits already know what is in store for us. We've been waiting for this. Your presence, your existence, gives us hope. We know who you really are, Yemaya. We know you will go on. We know that you will teach the people our stories."

"What about your warriors?" I ask. "Why won't they fight?"

"My child, you are going into the vision that was meant for you only. Please respect our ancestors and say no more."

How can she choose this fate for her people? There are strong men and women who can defend their village. Although I am furious, I respect Cora's wishes and keep my mouth shut.

She gently tips my chin up toward the sky. "For every story, there is a beginning and an end. And every ending is the beginning of a new story."

The chill of this truth fills my body and leaves tiny bumps all over my skin.

Cora then tells me of my journey north to them. Her wrinkles form into a smile as she recounts my passage: "Our sister nation on the coast found you and brought you to us. They rely on the big water for food. One day, while searching for fish, a young man came upon something that looked like an overgrown gourd floating in the waves."

I must have dislodged from the wooden column.

"The visions, for me, had already started," Cora said. "The ancestors told me that I must impart all of my wisdom to you. If breath forms words, I must tell them to you."

My eyes grow large with insecurity and unworthiness. *Why does she believe I should bear this knowledge?* The elder knows my thoughts but does not waste her breath on my fear.

"As it was told to me, the elders of our sister nation had the same vision and knew of your coming before your arrival. The ancestors told them that their people must take the long journey from the coast and bring you to me. In eleven days' time, they arrived. Your cocoon was tied to a sturdy log that two men carried, one in front and one in back. The men stayed for a great feast and celebration that night and began their journey home the next day. We kept you in the middle of the village for the remainder of your metamorphosis."

I have so many questions, but she holds up her ancient hand to stop me. "There still is much I must share with you."

She continues, although I see her body is weary. "The precious little one Ozata, my granddaughter, made the Mer figurine for you." Cora rubs her hands together as if to massage her aching bones. "She knew what you were before any of us. I was certain that she would become your guardian. Ozata is young, only seven years old, but she will soon undergo her rite of passage. Most of the tribe does it at ten years, but I had a vision that she must go in her seventh year."

"What is her rite of passage?"

She clears her throat. "Ozata will sleep overnight in the forest alone, bringing no weapons."

Cora senses my concern and adds, "She is more than capable of surviving."

"When will she go into the forest?"

"Tonight."

My mind floods with visions of all the dangers she might encounter. "How will she defend herself?"

Cora smiles. "*If* she has to defend herself, it will be with weapons or tools that she creates herself."

I rub my face to help clear my mind. "Why does she have to do this?"

"My child, we cannot truly know ourselves if we do not go through this rite. No one can tell you how to mature; you have to experience it yourself. What Ozata experiences tonight will give her the wings she needs to fly."

Cora's words make sense, but I still do not see the logic in testing such a young child. Especially if failure means death. I sit, stewing in my emotions.

"How old are you?" Cora asks.

"Seventeen."

"And did you not go through your own rite of passage as a child? Did you not learn that you could survive on your own?"

"Yes," I say, bowing my head, "but I did not choose to." I choke up, thinking of my parents.

"Sometimes it is not our choice; Great Spirit always has a plan."

I cling to her words because the pain of my past is too heavy to hold. I still feel weak from the plant medicine. Cora gently embraces me as I fall into a deep sleep.

I awaken to the sounds of the flute. Night has set, and I am alone. A bonfire in the middle of the village creates silhouettes of the tribe dancing upon the walls of the huge tent. I make out Cora. Her shadowy figure slowly shrinks as she approaches the hut. I attempt to get out of bed, but I am weak. As I try to prop myself up, my arm collapses beneath the weight of my body.

Cora enters with fresh water from the stream. "You are awake."

She gently pulls my arm out from beneath me. She holds my head up and pours a small amount of water into my mouth. It seems to evaporate before I can swallow. I feel my strength returning more quickly than I thought it would.

"This evening, while you were sleeping, Ozata went into the forest. She has asked that you be the one to retrieve her in the morning. You can go when your body is ready."

She pats the fresh water on my forehead with a wet cloth, and I feel a surge of energy.

Cora explains, "They play the flute to remind Ozata that although she is alone in the forest, we are always nearby. The men will take turns throughout the night playing different tunes to comfort her." She gathers the water gourd and folds the cloth she used to cool me. "Listen to the wisdom of the child. She is clear, free from self-interest and manipulation. She requests that you be the one to retrieve her," she repeats. "She knows that she will be alive in the morning. She needs your faith. She needs you to know that she will make it through the night. You must rest. You will stay with me tonight."

I comply.

4

RITE OF PASSAGE

I lie awake, aware of every sound. My mind will not allow sleep to distract me from my worries. The night is long. Nocturnal animals move just outside the tent's walls. I hear the crawling of insects across the ceiling. The air cools with each passing hour, and I pull my blanket up from my feet to wrap around me.

Never have I experienced a longer night. I try to close my eyes, but the sound of drums and nature's shadowy percussion constantly startle me. The flute welcomes the first rays of sun with a change in tune. Staccato notes mirror the tribe's excitement for Ozata's journey coming to an end.

Cora's wrinkled face has grown weary over the course of the night. She has been up as well, praying and chanting for the child. As I sit up, I notice an intricate design of colored sand painted on the floor. It was not there when I saw Cora's home in the daylight. She must have created it after we entered last night.

"It's a sand painting. We use it in ceremony. This one is to protect Ozata and bring her clarity of purpose."

"It's beautiful."

She wipes the extra sand off her hands and says, "It is time."

"But where do I go? Where is she?" I ask as I carefully step around the delicate painting.

"I will show you where she began her journey, but as you venture deeper into the forest, Great Spirit will send you signs. You must pay close attention to them, and follow the guidance you receive," Cora says quietly.

"Who is Great Spirit?"

"Great Spirit is the force that watches over and protects us all. Animals, plants, trees, and fire. The water, the rocks, and all the flowers. Everything."

Cora places a small leather bag around my neck. "This medicine pouch will protect you as well. There is sage, an arrowhead made of onyx, and the figurine that Ozata crafted." She picks up two brown objects from the floor and says, "You must put these moccasins on your feet to protect you from sharp sticks and rocks, as well as wet weather. You will get used to them quickly and they will help you move faster and with more confidence in the forest."

I take the moccasins from her and admire their exquisite craftsmanship. They are embellished with sparkling blue beads that have been sewn onto their sides to create the shape of ocean waves. Cora gently takes them from me, motions for me to sit, and helps me fit them on my feet.

She smiles and says, "The waves will remind you of your power as a Mer."

Cora kisses my forehead, fits a bundle with a fur blanket for sleeping and a pouch with food on my back, and leads me into the gathering of trees at the entrance to the forest. I navigate through and around the dense foliage. Masses of tangled branches and vines connect the mighty trees, creating a canopy over my head, which shelters me from the heat of the rising sun. The air is thick with life, from minuscule insects to mighty birds circling above. Small furry animals jump from tree to tree, oblivious to any potential danger.

I can still hear the flute. The sound that is meant to comfort Ozata is doing the same for me. I realize that the music is our guiding light and that we can follow the sound of the melodies back home.

I hear a rustle in the leaves. My attention focuses in the direction of the sound. My vision sharpens, and I catch sight of a panther in the distance. We stare at each other, still and silent. Unlike in my dream, I am terrified. This mighty beast can finish me with one swipe of her paw. She turns and runs deeper into the forest. *Is this a sign? Is this even real?* I cautiously begin to follow her. As thought catches up with my body, I am reminded of my vision. I ran after Obatala in the same way. My medicine animal disappears into the morning mist.

I find myself standing in the middle of a small clearing. The undergrowth has been visibly disturbed. A patch of branches partially covers a large hole in the rich earth.

"I'm here," a voice calls from the trees.

I smile as Ozata makes her way down the trunk of a large tree with hanging branches. "That was fast," she says. "I thought I'd be waiting all day for you."

"Thanks for your faith in me," I retort. Once she hits the ground, she jumps and hugs me.

"Let's eat before we begin our journey back," I suggest.

Ozata smiles broadly and nods. "I survived, but I didn't find anything to eat. Good thing it was only for one night," she says through laughter.

I pull out my pouch and hand her a piece of flatbread. We sit on the forest floor. She seems even smaller surrounded by the vast wilderness. She leans forward and breaks off a fairly large piece of the bread, eating it quickly. Before she swallows the last bite, she grabs a carved stick and commands, "Come on!"

"What's that?"

"This is my weapon. I hollowed the stick in the same way that my grandfather showed me how to make a flute. I sharpened a smaller stick and soaked it in the poison of the everplant. I had to be ready just in case."

We follow the sound of the flute through the

forest. Where I stumble and trip, Ozata glides gracefully. Her movements are skillful and elegant, almost as if she were swimming through the legions of mighty oaks.

"Does this look familiar?" she asks.

"It all looks like the same forest, but I cannot tell if we've passed this tree."

"Look," she says, showing me a carving on a tree trunk, "I made these marks on the way into the forest to point me home."

I trace the marking with my fingertips and recognize the mastery it took to create it. Cora shared with me some of their symbols and their meanings. Ozata had carved a bear track, which represents a good omen.

"So beautiful," I exclaim. Ozata smiles at my appreciation.

Suddenly the sound of the flute stops.

"Maybe they're starting a new song," I say hopefully.

"No. He didn't finish the last one. Something's wrong."

Ozata grabs my hand and leads me through the forest toward the village. She checks the marked trees to verify our direction. There is a circle representing life, a rattlesnake jaw representing strength, and crossing arrows representing friendship.

We run without rest through the trees and brush. I mimic her every move, and we navigate through the forest as one, swift and light. A loud blast in the distance stops us in our tracks.

"The white man," she whispers.

The familiar sound of gunshots reminds me of the horrors I witnessed on the ships. Ozata starts to run toward the village. I pull her back.

"Let go!" she cries. "Mama! Mama!"

She breaks free from my grasp and races toward the tents, barely visible through the tangled web of trees and vines. I follow her.

As we near the village, we hear several more guns fire.

"Stop!" she shouts in the white man's tongue.

One of the men hears her and looks toward us. He yells to the others and begins the chase. I pull Ozata into my arms to keep her from running into the village. She is small and extremely lean. I can move swiftly carrying her, even though she fights my grip. I know I can't let her go back. We will both surely die if I do.

Miraculously, I navigate through the thick forest. What once seemed like scattered randomness now feels like a map guiding me to the clearing. I recognize the plants and formations.

She whispers in my ear, "I'm fine now, you can put me down. I won't go back."

Her feet hit the ground without missing a step, and she manages to run alongside me without stumbling. Effortlessly, she veers to my left and passes me.

"Wait, not that way!" I yell.

"Follow me!"

The underbrush seems to multiply as we delve deeper into the forest. Eventually, I recognize our location. We circle the clearing that she created the night before. I hear a sound behind me and look over my shoulder. I fall unexpectedly through the branch-covered hole. Piercing pain shoots through my ankle.

Ozata hears me shriek in agony, and she turns around to help me out of the hole. When she realizes I can't move, she motions for me to get down, tucks me in, and covers me with twigs and leaves. She whispers, "Don't make a sound."

Through the leaves, I catch a glimpse of her climbing the tree I found her in earlier this morning.

As she moves out of sight, I become aware of my surroundings. The cool, damp earth around me is fragrant with various minerals and lumpy with tree roots. My ankle aches. The pain feels like a shark has sunk his teeth into me. I bite my lip to keep from weeping.

A twig snaps. Someone is here.

Suddenly I can hear my own breathing, like a very large animal panting in my ear. I hold my next inhalation as the man approaches my hideout. Through the scattered branches I can see that he is pointing his gun in my direction. He moves slowly toward me, crackling the cover of the forest floor with each move. Without warning, he collapses to the ground. One of his lifeless blue eyes stares at me through the sparse leaves.

Ozata jumps from the tree and pulls away the greenery that covers my hole. The throbbing in my ankle is almost unbearable. I throw my head back in pain and say loudly, "I can't move!"

Ozata removes her poison dart from the man's neck. She grabs his gun and peeks into the hole. "We have to go now, before the others find us."

"Just leave me."

"Come on," she says as she tucks away her weapons. She reaches in and attempts to pull me out. "Use your good leg."

I hold on to her firm grip and use my healthy leg to maneuver myself out of the hole.

"I know a cave we can stay in for the night," she says.

She reaches up and attempts to help me steady myself so that I can move forward. I notice that there is blood on her fingers. As I stand up straight, she lowers her arms and wipes the blood from her hands onto her leather covering. Rust-colored stains mar the innocence of her small beaded dress. We move forward without saying a word.

It seems that this is Ozata's true rite of passage. She has gone from being a little girl to being a warrior. All of the wisdom that Cora shared with me is beginning to make sense. She knew that we would survive. She knew that we would be the ones to carry the village's flame.

We run for what feels like days but the sun never sets. I fear I might pass out from the pain.

"We're here," Ozata says at last.

I see no cave. Ozata marches through the greenery. I nearly collapse on a bed of sharp rocks, but I catch myself by grabbing on to a young tree. I regain my balance and focus my attention ahead. Camouflaged in the forest vines is a moss-covered grotto. It is smaller than I had imagined.

"We'll be safe here. The river is just behind us."

Ozata crawls into the cave and motions for me to follow. Instead, I hobble past the opening and make my way toward a large boulder. I lean on the rock and lift my injured ankle up slightly so I can examine the damage. It's quite swollen and there are tiny weblike fibers growing out of and around the injured area. I brush them away and gently place my foot back on the ground.

I peer over the jagged edge of the boulder and see that down at the bottom of a shallow hill a river flows through the trees. It is not far from us, and droplets of river water splash against my body, unexpectedly imbuing me with a sense of power. My entire being is drinking up the water.

My grip on the boulder tightens and a piece

of the granite cracks between my fingers. I stare in wonder as the powdery fragments crumble to the forest floor, creating a thin layer of white dust.

"Go to the water. It is calling you," Ozata urges.

She scrambles out of the cave and guides me down the narrow path to the river. Miniature frogs leap from the trail and into the overgrown grass. A slight smile peeks through her soiled face.

"Thank you," she murmurs.

"But you saved me."

"We saved each other," she says as she reaches down to wash the blood from her hands in the river.

I lower my body into the gently flowing water. My eyes close as I imagine myself swimming freely in the deep waters of the ocean. The crisp temperature of the stream surrounds me with nostalgia. Although the pain in my ankle remains, the water serves as a considerable distraction. I submerge myself fully in the river. The pores in my skin pull the oxygen from the stream, allowing me to stay under without needing to take a breath. After a few minutes underwater, I open my eyes and spot the distorted image of Ozata peering down at me from the riverbank. I sit up and shake my hair.

"You haven't lost all of your powers," Ozata points out. "You can still breathe underwater."

Her face reddens as she looks down and starts twirling the leather pieces hanging from the bottom of her dress.

"Ozata." I beckon her. She looks at me, and I open my arms. Without hesitation, she jumps in the water. We cling to each other, grateful to be alive. I tighten my embrace as she begins to cry. She buries her head against my shoulder.

5

TAKE SHELTER

Ozata and I fall asleep for the night.

"Wake up," a deep voice whispers in the language of the white man.

Jerking my eyes open, I see a man bending over me. *Is he a pirate?* I reach for Ozata, but she's gone.

"Where is she?" I push the man with all my might. "Where's Ozata?"

Staggering backward, the man blurts out, "Settle down. I won't hurt you. Ozata is with her mother, outside by the river."

I hop to the opening of the cave and see Ozata where he said she was. I'm relieved, but then I turn back toward the white man. "What do you want?"

"I want to help you," he says. "I'm from the Society of Friends."

His words mean nothing to me.

"I'm a Quaker."

"What is that?"

"I'll explain later," he says. "I can help you."

"How?"

"I'm a doctor," he says. He reaches for

something in his bag, then shows me some short sticks and a roll of white cloth. "I'm like a medicine man. You broke your ankle. Let me wrap it with this cloth. It will take a while to heal."

I shake my head in disbelief.

"You'll be fine, but I must bandage your ankle quickly."

I look at my ankle and again see tiny webs growing out of the injured area. I make my way back to the fur blanket and ease my body down. I'm careful to brush the fibers away from my ankle, without drawing attention to what I'm doing. The man doesn't move toward me until I nod. He begins to wrap my ankle, and the pain is so intense that I grip my blanket to keep from screaming.

He hands me a small twig and tells me to bite it. "It'll help with the pain."

"Why are you doing this?"

"A Quaker believes that all life is sacred and equal. I'm sure you have many questions for me, but I don't have time to explain now. I'll tell you everything later, I promise. Our carriage is waiting at the edge of the forest."

He offers his hands, indicating that he wants to help me walk. "May I?"

It becomes clear that he means to carry me.

I recoil slightly, and he stops. "We must get out of here now if we are to survive. Your broken ankle will slow us down—so let me assist you. Please."

I nod, and he lifts me off my feet and swoops me out of the cave.

"We must hurry," he calls to Ozata and her mother.

They run up behind us as we make our way through the forest. Amitola reaches for my hand and squeezes it. I'm too scared to ask what happened to Cora.

We dart through the trees until we get to a clearing where a horse, hooked up to something that looks like a wooden box on steel circles, awaits our arrival. I guess this is the "carriage" that the white man mentioned earlier.

He lays me gently on the floor of the carriage and covers me with a blanket. "Sorry, but not many people around here share my beliefs. I have to conceal your presence until we reach my property line. They will not question the Natives," he says as he seats Ozata and her mother inside the carriage with me. "They will think we are making a trade."

He moves to the front of the carriage, pulls on some leather straps attached to the horse, and talks to it to get it to move. A large crack between the wooden panels that make up the carriage allows me to spy ahead of us. I cover my ears when I hear the horse, remembering the ones that were used to tear Obatala's friend apart.

The monotonous rhythm of the carriage over the path lulls me nearly to sleep. A few miles down the road, the pattern from the steel circles changes. I peek from under the blanket.

"I think we're here," Ozata whispers.

The Quaker stops the carriage and walks back to us. "Welcome," he says as he opens the door.

He reaches in to lift me up and out. We step on a beautiful, soft green expanse lined with weeping willows and great oaks. I remember Cora telling me the names of these particular trees. The willows are my favorite.

"You're free to roam here," he says. "I rarely have visitors."

In spite of his words, Ozata clings to her mother, and Amitola comforts her.

I look at Amitola and ask, "Where's Cora?"

"She's alive, but I must explain later," she says as she attempts to cover Ozata's ears.

I shudder and look out across the small hill, toward the white man's home. It is large, maybe ten times bigger than Cora's tent. There are many different levels, with regular rows of dark, shiny squares on each floor that reflect the bright sunlight. An outdoor wooden floor protected by an overhanging roof wraps around the front of the house. I notice many beautiful flowering plants in clay containers positioned all around the outdoor floor. To the side of the main door are a table and wicker chairs. Cora had a similar chair that she said she traded five baskets for.

The white man encourages me to lean on his arm as we walk slowly toward his grand house. I take his hand as he patiently leads me up through his trees.

We enter the house and an African man dressed almost exactly like this white man rushes to assist him. I turn toward the white man in confusion.

"He is paid a wage," he says.

I have no idea what he's talking about. I look at the African man and ask in the language Obatala speaks, "Do you know where Obatala is?"

The man frowns at me and looks at the white man, who indicates that he should leave. Without answering my question, the African man walks out of the room. I am more confused. The white man leads us into another room, where we sit at a round table. He puts a small chair without a back next to me and gently places my leg with the bandaged ankle on it.

Crouching at my feet, he smiles up at me and says softly, "I am Richard Dillingham. What is your name?"

An African woman with skin lighter than mine, covered completely by a heavy, stiff-looking floor-length dress, walks up to the table. Richard looks at her and says, "Sara, please bring us some tea."

Richard does not move from his place next to my feet and continues to gaze at me. He says, "I can't put my finger on it, but you are different."

I'm not interested in having this conversation. I just want to know what happened to Cora and the rest of the tribe. I work up my nerve and ask Amitola, "Is Cora safe? And the others?"

Amitola speaks to me in her native tongue. "We must tell you something."

"I was getting to that," Richard says in her language.

I am amazed to hear the white man reply to her with the words Cora so lovingly taught me.

Sara walks in with her chin slightly raised. She doesn't look at anyone as she places down a tray with shiny small cups and a larger jug of some sort. I can't help but notice how similar the material is to the hard ropes that shackled Obatala and his people. Ozata jumps on my lap, waking me from my dark study.

I can tell that Amitola is dreading what she has to say. "We are going to stay with another nation, just north of us."

Sara drops one of the hard cups and it rolls to my injured ankle. She looks as if she might cry as she trips over her dress to fetch it. "Pardon me," she says as she scurries out of the room.

My hands shake as I ask, "But what happened to everyone? Why do we have to go there?"

Ozata looks into my eyes and says very gently, "You cannot come. This nation is not as open to your people as we are."

"Some even own slaves," Richard adds as he stands to pour the tea that Sara has left on the table. "It might be best if you stay with me until you are healed."

What are slaves? I retain my questions because all of this talk seems to pull me further away from Obatala.

"I can't. I'm looking for someone." I glance at Amitola.

Amitola says, "The other survivors of the raid are already on their way there. We'll live with the other nation until it's safe to return. During the raid, I hid and eventually escaped. I was determined to find you and Ozata."

My heart is pounding as I ask, "What about Cora?"

Amitola says, "She's safe. She's with the others on her way up north."

I put my arms around Ozata and hug her tight.

"You must go. That's what's best. I'll be fine," I whisper to Ozata.

"I know," she responds.

They leave in the morning. I don't expect that I will ever see them again, but I lie to myself as I hug my little angel. "I will see you soon."

Ozata touches my medicine pouch and says, "We're always with you. You have all the medicine you need to find Obatala."

Richard and I watch from the doorway as two

white men help Ozata and her mother mount a horse. Ozata looks back at me and clutches her medicine pouch around her neck. She smiles and holds her mother's waist as they ride off with the men.

Richard leads me back into the room where we had the tea. "I'm sorry that it has to be this way."

I am silent.

"Where did you come from?"

I shrug my shoulders.

"I can see that you are in no mood to talk. Do you mind if I do? I hate to break this to you right now, but I have to go to Tennessee for a couple of days. I leave later on this evening, but the staff will take care of you."

I smile to acknowledge his words, but honestly, I am relieved. This is the first time I've had to hide my true nature. He would never understand. I look at him, and it is almost as if I am seeing him for the first time. His eyes look like the crystal-clear waters of the ocean and his hair is as black as the onyx arrowhead I have in my medicine pouch. He is gentle, his touch nurturing and kind.

"I don't know if I've thanked you yet," I say just above a whisper.

"No need for that, please. Pardon me," he says, "I'll be right back."

Richard leaves the room. I take in the beauty and mastery of the structure: the intricate designs on the walls, the sparkling stones hanging from the lights on the ceiling, and the large, soft chairs that take up half the room.

Sara enters and interrupts my thoughts. "Excuse me," she says harshly as she slams down a tray of food in front of me, then stares at me.

I don't know why she is angry, but I want to know more about her. "Are you African?" I ask in Obatala's tongue.

Sara is silent and rigid. I try in the language of the white man.

"Did you come on the ships?"

"No, of course not. I used to work for Richard's godfather, and whenever he would visit, Richard would request that I get the day off so I could play with him. He has been my best friend for as long as I can recall. He is not like most other white men."

"Yes, I see that."

"Don't get too comfortable," she says as she exits the room.

Richards returns with new bandages and ointment. "Here are some supplies. I should return before you need more."

"Where is Tennessee? Why are you going there?"

"Do you know what the Underground Railroad is?"

"No."

"You speak as if you have been here for years,

were maybe even born here. Yet you are ignorant of so much."

"Cora taught me her ways and the tongue of the white man."

Richard nods. "The Underground Railroad is a network of safe houses and secret passages and routes for Negroes to escape slavery and flee up north to free states or Canada," he explains.

He can see that I am confused. *What is slavery? Is "Negro" another word for "African"?* I have too many questions to even begin to understand.

"Did you come through the Middle Passage?"

"I'm not sure."

"Did you come on the slave ships from Africa?"

"Something like that. I would rather not talk about it."

Richard shakes his head. "I do not know when this nonsense will cease. This type of trading was supposed to stop long before I was born."

He drops the bandages on the floor, and we both reach down to retrieve them. Our eyes meet. The rich blue reminds me of my yearning for the ocean. He is beautiful. His skin is light olive with faint freckles close to his nose, and his lips are thin but full. His face reddens all of a sudden as he backs away. "I'm sorry," he mumbles, grabbing up the bandages as he stands.

I look up and see Sara across the room, hovering by the door. How long has she been there? Richard notices that my gaze has shifted.

He turns around and sees Sara. She ducks her head and disappears back through the doorway.

I look at Richard and ask, "Can I tell you something? I did come on the slave ships. There were three of them." I pause for a moment, remembering that horrifying journey. "I came with someone I was in love with, but when we got here, we were separated. I ran away and was rescued by Amitola's tribe. They took care of me and taught me all I know. Do you think Sara or someone else here might know where he is?"

I touch the back of my neck and add, "His name is Obatala. He has three scars on the back of his neck."

Richard stops me. "John!"

"Excuse me?"

"You speak of John . . . Obatala. He came on the ships earlier this year," he explains. "He's at a plantation near here."

"You know him? Can you take me there?"

"It is getting late. I will take you to John— Obatala, as you call him—when I return. Your leg has to heal before you can travel anywhere. Promise me you will not leave this property while I'm gone. The men in this area are extremely violent with the African people."

I nod, but I know that I will leave in the morning to find Obatala. Although I feel an overpowering yearning to see him, I need to sleep first so that I have the strength to find him. My mind races, and it feels like angelfish are fluttering in my stomach.

"I must ready for my journey," Richard says as he gathers his things. "Sara will take good care of you while I'm gone."

6

BETRAYAL

Richard sets off as the sky darkens. From the chair on the porch, I watch his horse and carriage disappear into the distance. I take in the beauty of the land around me. Grass-covered meadows surround his house. There is a small lake in the distance that I hadn't noticed before. I long to be near the water, to slide in and swim. I wonder how it would feel without my tail.

Sara approaches me from the dark interior of the house. "Are you hungry?"

"No, thank you."

I can see she is angered by my presence, but I'm too exhausted to ask her why. My ankle is throbbing, and I just need to sleep.

"I would like to lie down, to sleep. Would you help me inside, please?"

Sara hesitantly offers her arm, which I gratefully take. She guides me to the guest room, and before she closes my door, she says, "Your sleeping clothes are laid out on the bed. Let me know if you need anything else."

I nod as she exits the room. I feel too tired to change into the nightclothes, but I'm still dressed in the thin leather shift Cora gave me three days ago. I'm beginning to shiver with cold, and the white nightgown looks soft and warm. I pull the shift off and slip the heavy gown over my head. I poke my hands through the long sleeves and smooth the dress over my body. The fabric falls all the way to the floor and makes me feel as though I'm snug and safe back in my cocoon. I tuck myself under the fluffy bedcovers and fall asleep before my head hits the pillow.

The sounds of loud barking and men yelling pull me from my slumber. I'm disoriented and cannot remember where I am. As soon as I recall, the door bursts open. Three red-faced white men rush into my room and pull me from the bed. My ankle hits the floor, causing me to scream in pain.

I look around and notice Sara standing in the corner of the room with her arms crossed. She stares at the floor.

"Sara?" I implore. She refuses to look at me.

"You thought you could run away, nigger!" The enraged men sputter saliva in my face as they continue yelling in my ear.

They drag me out of the house and throw me on the porch. I can see the illuminated faces of about six other men. They are carrying torches and waiting with their horses nearby. A tall man walks up to me, slaps me with all of his might, slings me over his shoulder, strides down the steps to his dancing horse, and throws me like a sack close to the horse's neck. It knocks the wind out of me, and I gasp as I feel him wrench my arms behind my back and tie my wrists tightly together.

In spite of the excruciating pain in my ankle, I kick my legs in an attempt to push him away and propel myself off the horse. He catches my legs and binds my ankles together. I hear the other men laughing as the tall man mounts his horse. He holds me against the saddle as we gallop away from Richard's house. His gang follows closely behind. My body flops against the horse's back as tree branches whip my face. I'm about to pass out when the men suddenly stop their horses midstride.

They are yelling and cursing. "Holy mother of God!" I hear the tall man gasp as he pulls up his horse, causing my body to slip. He catches my dress and yanks me back over the horse's neck. I start coughing and gagging. Thick clouds of smoke engulf us, almost blinding us to the horrific scene. I can see bodies lying everywhere, scattered across a lawn. I squint against the smoke and look toward the fire. I can recognize the skeleton of a mighty house completely consumed by flames. African men and women run screaming across the lawn and disappear into the forest. Is Obatala with them? They are far away, and the smoke is too thick for me to make out their faces.

An older white man, bleeding from his chest, startles me as he staggers up to the men on horseback. "Slave uprising," he stutters as he falls to the ground, blood pouring from his mouth, then he chokes out, "Hang them!"

The men wrench the horses around and kick them hard in the flanks. We take off down the road, and I fear I will never find Obatala. My ankle throbs unmercifully as the horses gain speed. *Where are we going? What will become of me?*

We gallop into what looks like a small village, with red and brown buildings lining a broad, hard-packed dirt road, dimly lit by tall treelike torches. As the men slow their horses, I notice that the village seems empty. I see no other people. Then I hear noises, music, yelling, laughing, coming from a nearby building. As we trot past the doors, a few white men walk outside and stare at us. They whisper and point when they spot me lying across the horse. We stop in front of a building that seems to be made of stone.

The tall man dismounts, pulls me off the horse, and throws me over his shoulder. He opens the door to the building and ushers the other men, still carrying their torches, toward the entrance. They drop their flaming sticks into buckets of water at the door. Smoke trails in after them. He unlocks a huge cage with thick metal bars separating it from the rest of the room and tosses me inside. As he slams the gate, he demands, "Whose nigger are you?"

I am silent. He growls at me, turns away, and motions for the men to gather around a heavy wooden table in the middle of the main part of the room. He looks at the man sitting at the table and says, "Sheriff." Then he looks at the men around him and says, "Gentlemen, we have a situation. Our niggers think they can get away with killing good, moral people. We have to travel to the surrounding townships and warn them about the uprising. The slaves will be heading north through Virginia. We have to tell everyone to be on the lookout for escaped slaves. All in favor say aye."

"Aye!" they all respond.

"Gather as many men as you can. We will leave in an hour," he proclaims as he slams his fist on the table. The men rush out, leaving me in the cage.

The night is dark, lit only by the thin crescent of the new moon. I unwrap my bandage and observe the swollen mass that once was my leg. As I lean in closer, I see that the tiny weblike hairs are growing out of my injured ankle again. Instead of wiping them away as I did before, I concentrate on the growing threads as they extend before my eyes. They wrap around my calf and foot. Millions of tiny strands secure my injured limb in place.

Mucus-like liquid slowly spews from my pores, and I rub it in around my self-made dressing. The mucus quickly hardens into a cast, and I can feel my bones heal almost instantaneously. I smash the cast on the floor to crack it off. I roll my ankle in a circle and then pull myself upright using the bars of the cage as support. I place my foot on the floor and put weight on it. I'm amazed that it doesn't hurt. I hold on to the bars of the cage and slowly lower myself to the floor.

Suddenly, thunder booms and lightning cracks across the sky. A torrential rain begins to fall. The window is slightly ajar, and water sprinkles in through the opening. The same strength that I felt at the river returns as the water seeps into my pores.

The door slams open and interrupts my solitude.

"That damn rain!" the man called Sheriff yells as he enters the building with a younger white man. "Light the lantern, it's too dark in here." The young man strikes a match and sets fire to the wick, flickering it to life.

Sheriff hollers out to the men on the street, "We'll set off come morning. By then the rain should cease."

He slams the door and pulls off his coat. "Damn!"

The other man takes his coat and hangs it on a wooden rack beside the door.

Sheriff turns toward me. "What are you looking at?"

He walks up to the bars and squints at me. "You're not a slave, are you?"

"No," I quietly respond.

He hits the bars in frustration, then turns toward his companion and says, "My brother got killed tonight at the plantation. Stabbed."

"Yes, sir, I know. It's a shame, a real shame."

"Someone will pay for this!" Sheriff breathes a deep sigh. "Our niggers are running wild. I need you to stay and watch this one overnight. I'll be back in the morning."

"Yes, sir. I just need to fetch a few things from home. Do you want to stay with her while I'm gone?"

"She'll be fine." Sheriff laughs. "She ain't going nowhere."

They leave the lantern burning as they exit the office, slamming the door shut behind them.

Suddenly, I remember the rock I crushed at the river. "Can I still do that?" I whisper into the night air. I firmly grip the iron bars, pulling them with all my might, but nothing happens. I am baffled. What has changed? The rain outside the window begins to intensify. Drops of water splash upon my skin. I feel renewed again. I grab the bars, and slowly the metal begins to give way. I pull them apart just wide enough to slip through, and I realize that I must be touching water to access my strength. As I step out of the cage, I hear the doorknob rattle. The younger man is back.

I quickly jump inside the cage and close the opening in the iron bars with the last bit of power in my body. My eyelids droop with exhaustion, and as they close over my eyes, I suffer a cruel hallucination. I blink to chase the image away, but Obatala remains in front of me. He caresses my cheek and whispers, "We will be together soon."

As I close my eyes again, I hear the man's footsteps approaching my cage. He stands there for a moment, his breathing labored and raspy. He walks away, and then I hear the scrape of a chair across the floor. I peek through one eye and see him sit at the table and pick up a pile of papers. As he sorts through them in the dim flickering lantern light, I close my eyes again and fall into a deep sleep.

I awaken to the rhythm of a herd of horses. I roll over on the dusty wooden floor and look through the bars of my cage. The room seems much bigger in the light of day. I am alone. The noise outside intensifies as men, women, and children begin shouting with angry excitement. Between indecipherable screams and shouts, I can hear them chanting, "Hang them all! Hang them all!"

The bars of my cage now seem like welcome protection. I lie motionless on the floor, trying to stay out of sight. Last night I hadn't noticed the large windows facing the main road. I am exposed. It would be so easy for someone outside to see me through the glass.

The knob rattles and the front door of the building flies open. The younger white man who was with me last night walks in. He shuts the door hard and secures it. I'm frozen in terror as he glances in my direction. He hurries to the windows and pulls heavy cloth coverings over them, blocking out the sunlight and the curious gazes of the people outside. I feel momentarily relieved. Maybe this white man will be kind, like Richard.

He sticks his hand in his jacket pocket and walks slowly toward me. He smiles slightly and says, "It took me all night to forge this."

He pulls a folded piece of paper out of his pocket and offers it to me through the bars. I don't move, so he urges in a gentle voice, "Go ahead, take it."

I unfold the paper, and as I examine it, he says, "You're probably wondering why I'd do something like this for someone I don't even know. Well, let's just say that you remind me of someone I couldn't help, someone I cared about."

I smile at him and look at the paper again. It's covered in beautiful squiggles that are arranged in ordered rows. I turn it upside down and examine it from all angles. I stare at the paper in my hands in confusion. I can't imagine why this man has given it to me.

"Can't you read?" the man asks with some annoyance. Then I see a smile form at the corners of his mouth. "It's your Certificate of Freedom." He reaches in and takes it from me. "Here, see? Let me read it for you."

He clears his throat, takes a breath, and continues with an air of seriousness: " 'This is to certify to whomever it may concern that . . .' " He stops.

The young man hurries to his desk and retrieves a large feather. "What is your name?"

"Yemaya," I answer.

He dips the stiff end of the feather in a pot of thick black liquid, holds it over the paper, and mutters, " 'To whomever it may concern.' "

He scratches the paper with the feather. "Yemaya," he says. He ceases the scratching and resumes muttering, " 'A person of color, about seventeen years of age at five-feet-eight-inches high and of dark complexion, is a free person of color. I, T. M. William Brown' "—he stops muttering, looks at me, and winks—" 'have signed my name and affixed the seal of the court on this eleventh day of August in the year of our Lord one thousand, eight hundred, and forty-nine.' "

I am silent.

He frowns slightly and says, "Did you hear what I said?"

I nod and smile hesitantly, then whisper, "Thank you. Does this mean I can leave now?"

The man folds the paper and hands it to me. "Soon. Keep this document on your body. Anyone can ask you to prove your freedom. If you don't have it, you'll become a slave."

BANG!

The man slams into the bars. I jump backward and trip hard onto the floor. My ears ring for a moment, and then I go deaf as he collapses to the ground. His feet kick involuntarily. Blood pools beneath his body and seeps under the bars. I pull my feet in and quickly stuff my freedom paper into the pocket of my nightdress.

I can't hear the men break down the front door, but I can see their enraged purple faces and contorted lips yelling as they rush in and surround the dead man. They kick him and spit on him. Slowly, my hearing begins to return, and the sounds of them yelling, "Traitor!" echo throughout the room.

The dead man's blood slowly reaches my bare feet.

The men open my cage and two of them pull me up from where I'm crouching in the corner. We slip in the blood and slide across the floor. One of them hits his head on the bars and yells at me as he grabs me by my hair. The other one rummages through my pockets until he finds my freedom paper. He attempts to remove my nightdress, but I kick him with all my might. He flies back and slams into the bars. His fingers twitch as he slides to the floor. There is still breath in his lungs, but he looks dead.

The one gripping my hair stares at his companion in disbelief. After a moment of hesitation, he releases my locks and scurries out of the cage. The rest of the men are infuriated. They charge into the cage and tackle me to the floor. I feel the sharpness of their kicks and the bluntness of their blows until a cloud of thick white nothingness knocks me out.

7

UNLIKELY ALLY

I slowly wake up as I feel a warm, wet cloth cleansing the wounds on my face. I hesitate to open my eyes. The gentle strokes lead me to believe that I am safe.

"You don't need to open your eyes, but I can tell that you're awake," a soft female voice murmurs. I can hear her clearly, and I can even hear the warm water dripping into a basin as she wrings out the cloth. I'm relieved that my sense of hearing has returned, but the darkness around me makes me think I might now be blind. My eyelids lift to mere slits before the pain hits. I immediately close them again.

"You were beaten pretty badly. I convinced my uncle to leave you with me. Don't know what he and the other men would have done to you if I hadn't intervened."

Suddenly I remember: *My freedom paper!* I frantically begin to search for it. My eyes stay sealed shut as I toss about, feeling for it in each pocket of my nightdress.

"It's not there," she says. "The boys gave it to my uncle when he bought you. I'm not sure where he put it. Knowing him, it's probably long gone by now."

I throw my head back and immediately regret doing so. My pain worsens. *Where am I? Who is this woman taking care of me?*

She covers my body with a silken blanket and says, "I'm truly sorry about what they've done to you. The best thing for you right now is to get some sleep. I'll give you a change of clothes tomorrow. It's late. I must leave you for now, but I'm close by, in the room across the hall."

She sounds different from the other people I've met. I'm tempted to look at her, but the immense throbbing of my injuries stops me from trying to open my eyes again. The light in the room dims. I can tell because the shadows moving across my eyelids fade to black. I hear the woman pad softly away, the squeak of the door opening and closing, the rattle of the doorknob latching . . . and then the sickening sound of a lock clicking into place. *Why am I locked in? Where does she think I'll go? Am I her prisoner now?*

I can feel open gashes on my back sticking to my nightdress as I settle more deeply into the bed. In spite of my pain, I fall asleep almost immediately.

The morning sunlight hits my eyelids. I turn away from the light and open my eyes slowly, waiting for the agony to strike again. But the throbbing is gone! I reach for my face and feel the silken webs gently fall away. This time they are all over my body. I slip out of the bed and pull my crusty, bloodstained nightdress and underthings off. I examine my body as I wipe away the remaining webs. I reach around and feel the smooth, soft skin on my back. No gashes. I look at my arms, chest, and legs— no cuts or bruises. I feel my face and trace the familiar contours with my fingertips. No pain, no swelling.

The lock clicks and the door swings open before I can cover myself with the blanket.

"Oh my, good Lord!" the young lady cries as she slams the door shut. She stumbles toward me and dumps black boots, white cotton under-clothes, stockings, and a plain black-and-brown housedress in a heap on the bed. I jump up and back into a corner of the room, trying in vain to cover myself with my hands.

"This is a miracle," she whispers as she stares openly at my naked body. Her face reddens, and she turns away from me. "I'm sorry," she says as she grabs the dress and underclothes from the bed. She throws them in my direction and says, "Put these on. Quickly. No one can see that you are completely healed. How am I going to explain this?"

I pull on the clothing but am still fumbling with the buttons on the front of the dress when the young woman turns back toward me. At that moment I notice her delicate beauty. Her fine straw-colored hair, pulled back from her small face, reflects the sunlight streaming into the room, making her look as though she's glowing from within. She seems to be only a little older than me.

"Unbelievable," she says, walking cautiously toward me. "My God—how did you do this? Who are you?"

She peers tentatively into my face, then reaches up to stroke my cheek. I pull back, and she jerks her hand away. "I'm sorry."

She stands up straight, her posture becoming rigid. Her voice takes on a tone of authority. "We must not let them find you like this. They will think you're a witch." She hurries to the door and locks it, then motions to the boots, which are still on the bed. "Put those on."

I sit on the bed and pull the heavy boots over my thick stockings. The clothing feels oppressive and cumbersome, not like the soft, light shift Cora had given me.

"What is a witch?" My voice cracks and I realize these are the first words I've spoken to this young woman.

"A witch is a woman with magical powers. A sorceress." She moves closer to me and whispers, "Any woman who looks to nature for answers instead of our almighty Lord."

"A medicine woman?" I ask.

"Something like that."

Perhaps I am a witch.

"Your wounds, how did you . . ." She stops abruptly and laughs to herself. "Oh gosh, where are my manners? I'm always going on about something. You must be hungry. I will fetch you some food, and we can speak over breakfast."

She leaves the room without saying another word, and—as she did last night—she locks the door behind her. My stomach churns with the sound of the key turning in the lock, and again I wonder if I am her prisoner, or perhaps her slave.

The room, my new cage, looks like the bedroom in Richard's house. I stand and walk to the window, hoping that I might be able to climb out and run away before the young woman returns. *I must find Obatala before he goes too far away. Where am I? Where is he? Will I ever see him again?*

I hear a key unlocking the door, so I leap away from the window and am caught awkwardly lurching toward the bed when the young woman enters with a light-skinned African woman carrying my food. She reminds me of Sara, though she is older, and I wonder whether she will betray me as Sara did. I flinch slightly. She looks at me briefly before walking toward a small table perched next to a large, light blue chair by the bed. As the woman sets the tray of food down, she looks at the rumpled, bloodstained bedsheets, then up at my smooth, unmarked face, and murmurs, "Oh my!"

"Now, Margaret, I trust you won't say a word," the young lady chirps. I am struck by her tone. It is cheerful, but vaguely threatening. *Is Margaret her slave?*

"Of course not, miss," the serving woman replies as she begins stripping the stained sheets from the bed. She turns to me and says quietly, almost as if she doesn't want the young woman to hear, "Some of the field Negroes are saying that you're Yemaya."

"How do they know my name? Is Obatala here?"

At first she looks confused, but then her face softens as she bows slightly and answers, "They have been praying for you."

She gathers up the bedding and rushes out of the room before I can ask her anything else. The young woman immediately locks the door.

"They know you?"

"I don't know, but that is my name."

"This is so exciting," she exclaims. "I will be right back."

The door barely closes before the girl crashes back into the room with a leather-bound stack of papers.

"What is that?"

"It's my journal. Like a book with stories. I record all of my daily adventures in here."

I walk toward her to get a closer look at it, but she tilts the journal away from me.

I'm confused. I thought she wanted to show it to me. "I cannot read," I say to reassure her that I have no intention of prying into her private thoughts.

She clasps the book to her breast and cries out, "Oh, you poor soul. Reading is what I live for!"

Still holding her journal tightly, she kneels by the bed and pulls another book out from underneath it. "This was published when I was a child. My uncle would kill me if he knew I'd read it. I'm only allowed to read the Bible here. I hide it under the guest bed so he doesn't suspect it's mine. *The Hunchback of Notre-Dame*, by Victor Hugo," she says with reverence.

Her bright blue eyes light up. "I can teach you to read! I'm supposed to be nursing you anyway. I'll pretend you're still healing."

"I would love that, miss."

"Oh my, there I go again! Where are my manners? My name is Matilda Joslyn and I'm from Cicero, New York—everyone calls me Tillie. I'm only here in North Carolina until winter begins. I'm visiting my aunt and uncle." She ducks her head slightly and whispers conspiratorially, "Our house in New York is a station on the Underground Railroad."

"What is that?" I remember Richard trying to explain it to me.

"The Underground Railroad? You really don't know?"

"No, should I?"

"I'm so sorry. I thought you were mocking me," Tillie says as she carefully places her journal on the desk.

She keeps her voice low, but instead of pride, I detect a tone of fear and slight disdain. "My uncle Phineas owns slaves, so I have to be careful of what I say. He doesn't know that our house is a station."

"Is your uncle here?"

"This is his property, but don't worry, he promised you to me for my stay."

"Promised?"

"Like a gift. I know, it's simply awful. Barbaric. I'll be leaving here soon to go back home to New York, and there's no way I would be able to persuade him to allow you to come with me—even if I could pay for you—because he knows that I'd give you your freedom as soon as I got you out of the South." She goes on, "And if I voice my dismay, he'll likely take you away from me right now and make you a field slave, or sell you, or worse. Also, if I make too much noise about you and what he plans for you after I leave, he might start questioning my parents, and since our house is a station, he could get them into big trouble."

She says all of this at once, in a rush of words,

like a large ocean wave. "The Underground Railroad is really dangerous but necessary. It's a group of people who help runaway slaves get to freedom."

As I listen, my eyes drift toward the window, and then back toward Tillie.

She looks like a little girl, shy and ashamed, and I become afraid that she might start crying. She whispers, "Yemaya, please don't worry, I'm hatching a plan to get you out of here. My parents will be able to help us."

Tillie shakes her head and adds, "It's been going on for too long. They treat Africans like they are not human. They work all day, every day, with no pay. And the way they beat you—people like you. That's just normal. They beat them all like that. My uncle says that he is trying to make an example of the niggers who don't listen."

All of this information is just too much for me right now. I saw how they treated Obatala and his people on the ships. I stare out at the bright, hazy sky where I see black birds circling. I hear their caws and envy their freedom. *Where is Obatala right now? Perhaps he has made his way to the Underground Railroad.*

"Are you all right?" she asks.

"I'm just thinking about someone."

Tillie's eyes widen. "Who?"

"It's a long story."

"Oh, I love stories. Tell me, please."

Tillie hops on the bed, crosses her legs, and rubs her hands together.

"I came here on the slave ships."

I tell her about Obatala, about his scars, about how I knew him when we were children and how we reconnected before the pirates came. I tell her about what the pirates did to the tribe and how I was separated from Obatala when we landed in this country. I tell her everything except who I really am, my true nature.

Tillie sighs. "I'm so sorry. I can't even imagine what it must be like to have suffered the way you have."

She looks at me with sympathy, delicate tears forming in the corners of her eyes. "Your heart must ache so. We must find him. You must be reunited with your true love!" Tillie declares with determination. "However will we find him? How will we find Obatala? I wish I had a love like yours." She holds up *The Hunchback of Notre-Dame*. "This book is all about love."

She opens it and reads a passage: " 'Love is like a tree: it grows by itself, roots itself deeply in our being and continues to flourish over a heart in ruin. The inexplicable fact is that the blinder it is, the more tenacious it is. It is never stronger than when it is completely unreasonable.' "

She gazes at me and exclaims, "Let me teach you to read and write. That way you can write your epic tale, *after* we find Obatala and get you both to safety!"

I tell her that I am a fast learner, and we decide to start our lessons immediately. She reads the first page of *The Hunchback of Notre-Dame* to me while she points to the words.

"What are these symbols?" I ask.

"What symbols?"

I point to the many markings on the page.

"Oh, the letters. Do you know the alphabet?"

"No."

She pulls out her journal and writes down the alphabet. I use my memorization skills to learn the sounds of each letter. Within a few hours, I can sound out almost every word.

"Were you lying to me?" she inquires as she listens to me read about the beautiful gypsy woman, Esmeralda.

"I can learn almost as fast as I can heal."

She looks at me intently with a mixture of fear and awe. "What are you? I have never seen anyone like you, and I meet plenty of people." She laughs awkwardly and points to the eggs and oatmeal that made up my breakfast, which have become cold. "You really should eat; I'm sure you're famished. The food here is simply divine. I had them make my favorite: eggs Benedict and sweet oatmeal. It's cold, but still edible."

I realize at that moment that this food was made for her. "Did you give me your meal?"

"I'm not hungry. I don't eat much, and I knew you could use it."

This is my first meal since Richard's house. I eat it so quickly it gives me a stomachache.

"Do you want more?"

"Yes, please."

"I'll go fetch it for you." Tillie hides the book under the bed, hurries out, and forgets to lock the door.

I take the opportunity to sneak out into the long hallway. The ceilings are high, and the hanging lanterns emit only a dim light. Quietly, I close the door behind me. I have to find my freedom certificate. I see a library at the end of the hall.

There are many rooms with open doors. I tiptoe past them, and halfway down the hall, I hear a man's voice coming from one of the rooms I've already passed.

"Why do they always need me to approve the next move?"

I dash into the library and hide behind thick drapes covering windows that look out at a vast garden. My heart is pounding in my throat as I attempt to catch my breath. The man's voice approaches, then I see through a slight gap in the curtain two men, one African and one white, walk into the library. The white man must be Uncle Phineas.

"I lost three of my strongest slaves. But mark

my words, I'll get them back! If there is even a whisper about a slave revolt on my plantation, there will be hell to pay!" he yells. "Go tell the boys to ride without me. I have to stay and defend my turf."

"Yes, sir," the other man answers as he exits the room.

He must be a slave. I watch Tillie's uncle as he paces back and forth. I can almost hear his thoughts. He slams his fist on the massive oak desk. "Damn!"

He strides out of the room, and I take a deep breath that makes me choke and cough. The air is stale with the stench of . . . what? Smoke? And sweat. I step out from behind the heavy drapes and sit in front of the desk. I examine the many tiny drawers decorated with gold trim. My fingers wrap around the handle of the top drawer, and I open it.

Nothing.

I move to the second one and open it. There are loose papers. I carefully rummage through them, but there is no sign of my certificate.

"What are you doing?" Tillie asks in a frantic whisper.

I pull my hand back and shut the drawer. Tillie is standing in the doorway with a basket of fruit in her arms. *How could I be so careless?*

"My uncle will kill you if he finds you in here. Come with me and keep your head down, no matter what. Follow my lead," she orders as she grabs me up from her uncle's chair.

We make our way back down the dark hallway. Just before we enter the room, a woman demands, "Is that the Negro from last night?"

"Yes. We're on our way back to the room."

"You be careful now."

"I will, Auntie Soph."

Tillie pulls me along and shoves me into the room. This time she takes care to lock the door. "What were you doing?"

"I wanted to find my freedom certificate."

"I'm not sure if I made myself clear before, but my uncle is a very dangerous man. He has no qualms about murdering Negroes. No qualms at all! I will help you find your certificate. Just let me do the snooping."

She visibly softens. "I'm on your side, Yemaya. There are just a few games we have to play before we get your freedom back. I cannot pretend to imagine what it's like for you, but things are not perfect for me, either. When I'm older, I promise you that I'll change things for Negroes, Natives, and women. People always think I'm silly for thinking this way, but we're all in chains. I want to be free, too."

8

MAGIC

Tillie keeps me out of sight so no one will question why I have no wounds on my face or body. She stays in my room most days, pretending to nurse me. I have stopped counting the sunrises and my faith has seemed to dwindle.

Tonight, we stare at the waning moon, and Tillie asks, "Do you think the moon has anything to do with who we are as women?"

"Yes, I do."

"So do I. But whenever I try to talk about that with my mother, she says that I am speaking against the Bible. Sometimes she will let me talk, but I think she is afraid that I'm going to get myself hurt." Then Tillie confides, "I should just write a women's bible—that would be a controversy!"

"I would read it."

"After I was hanged. Or burned at the stake." She laughs a little.

"Why would they do that?"

"They have done terrible things to women for less than that: burning, torturing, drowning. All because some women think a bit differently. I'm so different that sometimes it scares me. I really think it may be me at the stake one day."

"Don't say such things!" Just as I'm about to reassure her, a distant sound grabs my attention. "Can you hear that?"

"No. What?"

"Drums. I definitely hear drums."

"Can you hear as well as you heal?"

I open the window and urge, "Come on."

"Wait! What are you doing?"

Smiling with anticipation, I pull my arm out of her grip and duck through the open window, swinging my legs up and out. As I slip down to the ground, Tillie scrambles to follow. We land on the plush damp grass.

The sweet, invigorating dew soaks my slippers as we hurry across the lawn. I feel my strength returning. I could run twice as fast now, but I would leave Tillie far behind. I match her pace and follow the faint sound of the drums.

"I hear them now!" Tillie exclaims.

"This way."

I grab Tillie's hand and pull her through the forest that surrounds Phineas's property. My eyes adjust easily to the dark, and I lead her through and around the dense trees. The run reminds me of the plant medicine, and suddenly I feel as if I'm back in that dream. I see the gleam of the panther's eyes peering at us from a high tree limb up ahead. I watch her warily, and as we run beneath the limb, I feel her breath on the back of my neck.

I stop suddenly, causing Tillie to crash into my back. She holds on to me as she steadies herself. I can feel her fear.

I whisper, "Follow me," as I take her hand and gently guide her deeper into the forest.

I can feel that Obatala is with me in spirit, guiding me, and as the drumming becomes louder, I am sure that I am being called. Tillie and I dart through the forest, avoiding trees and brush, sometimes stopping to get our bearings. The insistence of the drumming and its promise of something I do not yet understand keeps me from feeling my grief.

The pace of the drums seems to quicken as we approach the origin of the sound, but we can see nothing. We stop again. *Who is playing them?*

Tillie whispers, "Did they just say your name?"

We listen intently. There is a series of words I cannot understand, and then they sing my name clearly. Three times.

"They did!" Tillie proclaims.

I pull her toward the sound. A faint glow outlines the opening of a cave. The leaves and branches surrounding the area have been used as a barrier. We crawl around it and cautiously approach the mouth of the cave. It is covered with a thick blanket.

"My heart is going to beat right out of my chest!" Tillie exclaims.

"Shhh." I push the edge of the blanket aside so we can peek in.

Two African men are playing the drums while a group of men, women, and children dance around them. A woman dressed in blue and white takes a pull from a navy-colored bottle and spits the liquid on the dancers. They again chant my name. "Yemaya . . . Yemaya . . . Yemaya!"

The woman I recognize as the one who served me food, the one named Margaret, turns toward us. We quickly shut the curtain.

"Did she see us?"

"I don't know," Tillie answers, "but I'm not waiting around to find out!"

Before Tillie and I can run, Margaret appears and calls out, "Don't leave, Yemaya. We were expecting you. We have been praying to you to deliver us."

Tillie looks a little taken aback and asserts, "Margaret, what are you talking about?"

"Yemaya is the goddess of the ocean. She is the Mother of all Orishas. She is the Mother of all African people."

I am stunned to silence. She has it all wrong. I am not here to deliver anyone. I am just a fool out of the water, searching for Obatala.

"I must be the wrong Yemaya," I say.

Margaret falls to her knees. "It's you, I just know it. Deliver us! Deliver us!"

She begins to weep as Tillie pulls her to her feet.

"I saw the wounds you had," Margaret says, sniffling through her tears. "I saw them. There was blood and cuts and bruises. You were broken. Now look at you! How did you do it if you are not Yemaya?"

Tillie looks at me for an explanation as well. They both stare at me in wonderment. Their eyes are full of questions, but I cannot share my secret.

When I do not respond, Tillie turns to Margaret and asks, "Do you meet every night?"

"Only for one more day," Margaret answers. "By tomorrow night, we will have prayed for seven nights in all."

Seven. That's my favorite number.

"We know you love seven," Margaret says to me without question.

How does she know this?

"And blue is your favorite color."

I can't believe what she's saying. I haven't told these things to anyone.

Margaret no longer seems weak and defenseless. As she speaks of me, her voice becomes resilient and strong. Her conviction seems to intensify as she finally looks directly into my eyes.

"Remember who you are. Come with me.

Please." I move to follow Margaret, with Tillie right on my heels.

Margaret looks at Tillie, then says to me in a low voice, "She can't come in." I look back at Tillie, who has heard Margaret, and see that she is about to protest but then thinks better of it. She stops and with a wave of her hand encourages me to go in without her.

As I walk into the light in the center of the cave, gasps and awed exclamations fill the space.

"Yemaya?" the elder asks. She is stately and heavyset. The elder fixes her headwrap as she urges me to come forward. White garments almost entirely cover her body. Her face, neck, and hands are the only places where her glistening, yet wrinkled, skin is exposed.

"Yes, but—"

"Say no more, my child. Our prayers have been answered."

"*Asé*!" the crowd responds.

"I am not who you are looking for."

"We all saw what happened to you," the elder interjects powerfully as the crowd agrees. "The master whipped your unconscious body to a bloody pulp as an example of what he would do to us if we rose up. For all we knew, you was dead." She adds, "Your little friend out there saved your life."

I look toward the flap covering the cave and notice Tillie's blue eyes flashing through a crack in the curtain. Seeing Tillie's unrepentant boldness, I smile to myself, then nod to the elder.

"We prayed for you. Have you come to answer our prayers?"

I hesitate. Each person in this cave has placed their faith in my hands, and the weight of the burden is overwhelming. *I am not the One.*

"Ma'am, there must be some mistake."

"No," she declares simply.

I want to run, to get away from these people and their desperation, their expectations, their demands. I want to get away from these humans, be back in the ocean, swimming free.

"*You* are *the One.*" I hear Obatala's voice whisper in my ear.

I search the cave to see where he is, but it's clearly my imagination. There are seven candles flickering in the middle of the cave, and three pregnant women with their eyes closed sitting with their backs to the candles. The children have formed a circle facing the pregnant women, and the other adults have formed a circle around the children. They are all sitting except for the elder, whom I hear them refer to as Godmother.

"Welcome, Yemaya," she says.

At the sound of her voice, the three pregnant women rise and walk toward me. The circles yield to the women as they pass. They surround me and lead me to the middle of the group. They motion for me to sit.

A wave of emotion travels from my head down through my body. My skin ripples as I feel tiny bumps rise all over it.

Godmother begins to chant in an unfamiliar tongue. Her voice fills the entire space, leaving no room for wandering thoughts. Every person in the cave stands at attention. I attempt to stand up, too, but one of the pregnant women gently settles me back in my spot. The crowd sings back to Godmother. As she calls out, they respond in kind.

Suddenly they turn toward me, singing, "Yemaya, Yemaya, Yemaya."

As they chant, my eyes roll to the back of my head, and I begin to rock back and forth. My senses become hazy as my sight blurs, and sounds become distant, meaningless mumbles. The intoxicating scent of seawater surrounds me, and I taste something sweet and succulent. Watermelon?

That's when I lose consciousness.

9

RECOUNT

Silken sheets caress my skin as I turn in bed. *What happened?*

Tillie sits at the desk, avidly writing in her journal. She tucks a lock of blond hair behind her ear. She is in the same clothes she wore last night, the hem of her dress stained with dirt. I adjust my head on the pillow.

"You're up!" she cries as I stir. "Oh my dear God in heaven!"

"Was it that bad?"

"Bad? It was brilliant!"

"I thought you were not allowed in."

"What do you expect? There was only a wee curtain separating me from all of the action. Do you want me to read the details of the night to you?"

I settle in, knowing that her inquiry was a rhetorical question. She is going to read me the details—whether I want to hear them or not.

I have no recollection of the night beyond the initial song. Tillie begins to flip through pages. "Ah, here we are. Are you ready?"

"I think so," I say as I pull the sheets up to my chin. "Yes."

Tillie clears her throat and licks her pointer finger. " 'The Rebirth of Yemaya,' " she proudly proclaims. "I'll skip to when you started to rock back and forth."

"Yes, that is the last thing I remember."

Tillie begins reading from her journal. I am stunned to learn the many happenings of the night. There was a complete ceremony and, to top it off, I apparently went around telling everyone about their future. *How did this all happen?*

"Why don't I remember a thing? I just can't see how all of this could happen without me knowing!"

"I do not know how or why." Tillie shakes her head in disbelief. "But you became the Goddess that they spoke of."

"But if I became her, where was I? And who is she?"

"These are questions I cannot answer," Tillie says as she closes her notebook. "But you can ask Godmother tonight. She has asked us to join them for the final prayer of celebration. It will be by the river."

My first instinct is to say no.

"What are you thinking?" Tillie asks.

"I need to find Obatala."

"I know, I know, we must find your true love, but we have to go tonight. All of your questions will be answered. Your magic powers will come back to you in full, and we'll be more prepared to find him. I just know it!" Tillie proclaims.

"I'll go, but this time I want you with me."

"Of course! Once they saw how you, I mean *She,* acknowledged me, I was allowed to enter. I will be a part of the ceremony tonight."

Tillie turns back around and continues to write. I settle back against the down pillows, allowing my mind to wander. Suddenly, a flat image of three horizontal scars springs into my vision. His neck and then his back materialize before me, growing more solid, more real by the second. As I reach out to trace the familiar raised scars with my fingertips, he begins to walk away, eluding my touch.

"Are you all right?" Tillie interrupts.

The vision shatters into a million pieces, and it feels as if my heart follows suit. I slowly lower my outstretched hand.

"Why don't you rest," Tillie suggests. "I'll go to my room to write."

She smiles gently at me before she locks the door behind her.

This time, I understand that I am not her prisoner. She has locked me in to keep me safe. Nonetheless, I feel instantly desolate.

Silence.

Emptiness.

Loneliness.

The quiet leaves me victim to the voices in my head.

I am alone. I will never find Obatala. No one understands me. No one even knows who I really am. Everything is a struggle.

As I wallow in my self-pity, the hours seem to drag on. Eventually, the sinking sun touches the clouds with hues of fuchsia and lavender. I gaze listlessly at the silhouette of a large oak tree that stands starkly against the vivid backdrop. That tree looks so strong.

I am stirred by the succulent aromas of corn-bread, chicken, sweet yams, and collard greens that drift through the open window, pleasantly encircling me. Tonight, I know that the rich aromas are wafting over from the slave quarters. The contrast between my feelings of desolation and the joyful anticipation of the Africans who await my presence is painful for me. How can I possibly be the source of celebration when I feel so utterly lost?

I can no longer stand their expectation that I am here to deliver them. They are cooking the most extravagant meal that they can, with the little food they have. *Deliver them where, and to what? Do they think I can set them free? Do they think I have that power? I am proof that their prayers have been answered, but what can I really do for them?* I jump off the bed and hastily shut the window.

What if I am the one they are praying for? I am unlike anyone I have encountered thus far. *Could*

I actually be the Yemaya they worship? The possibility baffles me. Laughter ripples from my lips as I ponder myself as a Goddess.

I open the window back up. The sun has begun to set. Hanging branches of a willow tree sway in the warm breeze. The southern heat has seeped into the month of October. I close my eyes and I am transported back through time as I see my sacred medicine animal leading me to Obatala. He is sitting on the sands of our homeland, holding a bundle of blue-and-white flowers. The panther sits by his side. I swim in the waters a fair distance from the shore. Mother and Father float up behind me and lead me closer to Obatala. My beautiful tail morphs into human legs and I stand in the shallow waters with my parents by my side.

My father holds out the seventh shell, the one I never received, and motions for me to join Obatala. I slowly walk up to my love, halfway waiting for my dream state to disappear before I reach him, but it doesn't. I sit between him and the mighty beast, as he hands me the bushel of flowers.

"You are the *One,* Yemaya. They are already remembering who they really are. Just keep going. I will see you soon."

I reach out to embrace him and I slam my wrist on the windowsill in the guest room, snatching me out of my vision.

The door opens, and Tillie ushers Margaret into the room. Tillie has a basket of delicate blue-and-white wildflowers, which she sets on the bed. I say nothing of my vision, but seeing the blooms serves as a significant affirmation for me. Margaret stays by the door with her head bowed. Had I not witnessed her alter ego in the cave, I would not think it possible for this quiet lady to be so grand and proud.

"I am here to give you instructions for tonight," she says, just above a whisper.

I notice that she carries a white garment in her hands.

She holds up the plain-cut gown with large sleeves and says, "This is for you to wear." The dress hangs to my ankles, with enough material to flutter in the breeze. The neckline is embroidered with tiny blue flowers.

I take the dress into my arms and cradle it. "It is beautiful."

Tillie nods in agreement and says, "Now, that is fine craftsmanship! None of my dresses have ever been embroidered like that."

Margaret smiles thinly at Tillie and says, "A man will meet you both outside of your window in one hour. He will take you to the site." She then averts her eyes in deference once again. "Thank you, Yemaya. I knew it was you."

She bows and scurries out of the room. Tillie immediately locks the door behind her.

"You seem to be in brighter spirits," Tillie says, as she walks up to me.

"Yes, I feel much better. Thank you."

"Do you need help?" Tillie asks as I hold up the dress.

I take off my heavy garments and she slips the dress over my head. Tillie sits me in front of the mirror and wrangles my wild thatch of hair into a bun. She adorns my mane with the blue-and-white wildflowers she brought with her in the basket.

She places the final blossom on my head and says, "You look like a Goddess."

My own beauty catches me off guard.

Seeing the stunned look on my face, Tillie asks tentatively, with a tinge of insecurity, "Do you like it?"

"I love it." I turn to hug her.

"Mind yourself. You might wrinkle the gown."

The grandfather clock chimes and Tillie asks, "Are you ready?"

"Yes. Do you have your journal?"

"Dearie me! Thank you for reminding me. Wait here."

She runs out the door and sprints to her room.

I turn toward the mirror again to admire the work we have accomplished. Never have I seen myself in this light. I turn my head from side to side, taking in each angle. As I twirl around, I notice a small blue flower embroidered on the bottom hem at the back of the dress. I pull it up to get a better look.

The door bursts open and Tillie runs in, locking it behind her.

"Hurry," she whispers breathlessly. "Auntie Soph is looking for me."

Tillie dashes to the window. She holds out her hand to assist me down. We carefully gather the dress to keep from soiling the pristine white cloth. I jump to the ground and hold the hem in my hands.

"Watch out!" Tillie throws her journal out the window and follows closely behind. "We cannot stay here!" She grabs my hand and leads me into a nearby patch of trees. "It will be dark soon, and my aunt will assume I went to bed."

Tillie leans against a tree as she catches her breath.

"How are you going to write in your journal?"

"I borrowed my uncle's penner." She pulls out a small red leather container and flips open the rectangular contraption to reveal a miniature silver plume and ink container. "He would kill me if he knew I had it." She smiles as she closes it and slips it into a pocket. She holds the journal close to her chest and keeps a lookout.

We freeze as we hear a stick snap behind us. I can feel the hairs rise on the back of my neck.

"Yemaya?" a man's voice whispers.

We both release a long breath. "Yes," I say with a sense of relief.

The man emerges from the brush. I do not remember his face from last night. He is handsome and fit, with hair wild and free.

Tillie smiles as he approaches our hideout. "I remember you," she says. "What are you doing down south?"

"Yes." He smiles tightly. "We met last summer. Her parents are my colleagues," he says to me.

"Well, we mustn't keep them waiting," Tillie says.

The man lowers his gaze, saying, "Follow me."

The aroma from the feast seems to penetrate and overwhelm the natural smells of the forest. I hear a river babbling and gurgling in the distance. I hold my dress above my knees to avoid the mud from the recent rain. My naked feet are covered in the forest sludge.

Tillie notices the mud and gasps. "Yemaya! Where are your boots?"

Before I can reassure her that it's better for me to be barefoot, the man says, "We are almost there."

Tillie stops and turns toward me. She tucks an escaped tuft of hair back into my bun, then says, "You look beautiful."

I smile, remembering my reflection.

"Are you ready?" Tillie asks.

As ready as I'll ever be.

I realize that the man is patiently waiting for us. "I'm sorry," I say as we walk toward him.

"If I may be so bold, you are a sight to behold." I think I blush. "Thank you."

"This way, please." He ushers us toward the festivities.

As we approach the perimeter of the clearing, just past the slave quarters, the man begins a loud series of hand claps. Tillie and I stand behind him as he claps out several rhythms. Eventually, two drums join in with him and the crowd begins to chant, "Yemaya! Yemaya!"

"Follow me," he says as he moves toward the river.

I drop the hem of the dress and allow it to float in the warm breeze. Whispers and soft hums mix with the sound of the river to create a symphony of calming melodies. Everyone seems to carry either a bouquet or a garland of white flowers. Then I see Obatala, dressed in white. I rub my eyes, and the vision clears. Another man stands in his place, smiling and holding a bouquet of seven white roses.

Godmother is in the middle of the circle. She motions for the drums to cease with a flick of her right hand.

"Yemaya!" she bellows. "Your presence has renewed our faith and made us understand that no one can rob us of our roots."

The crowd cheers. I turn toward Tillie, and she

is applauding along with everyone else. Slowly, I raise my hand to speak. Several people in the crowd murmur, "Shhh, she speaks."

I clear my throat. "Even though we've only known each other for a short time, I have come to feel like we are family. And it is I who want to thank you. You have allowed me to see who I am." I look at each person standing before me. When my eyes meet Tillie's, we both tear up.

The crowd breaks out in whoops of appreciation again, some of them articulating their happiness with yelps and guttural utterings in their throats that erupt in ways that are uniquely and anciently African. The men begin to drum again. God-mother takes my arm and walks me toward the river. Tillie follows close behind, diligently writing with her uncle's penner.

"Go ahead, child," Godmother says as she motions for me to walk into the water. "I cannot follow you in. This must be your journey. Walk seven steps and turn around."

I look at Tillie. She nods and smiles confidently.

I take a deep breath and step into the gurgling river. My body drinks in the fresh water and is awakened by its primordial flow. As I take the next step, my feet are washed clean, and the bottom of the dress clings to my ankles. The third step brings the water to my knees. I am tempted to dive in and swim away. I bring my feet together with the fourth step, and I can feel all of my strength return to my body. My fifth step is small, because, with my soles and toes, I am feeling my way along the rocky riverbed. I go deeper with the next step, and the water rises to just below my waist. I turn around with my final step and face the crowd before me.

Someone has given Tillie a string of white flowers. She wraps them around her arm as she documents my every movement in her notebook.

The three pregnant women from the night before are at the forefront of the gathering. One woman is holding a string of flowers composed of mixed blue-and-white blossoms, another has a small watermelon, and the final one has a handful of pennies and a small wooden cup full of a dark liquid.

The rhythm of the drums changes, cueing the women to enter the river. The woman with the garland wades carefully toward me and hangs the string of blossoms around my neck. She says, "With these flowers, I honor the power of the ocean inside of you." The second woman approaches, and with great solemnity she places the watermelon in my hands and says, "With this watermelon, I acknowledge the infinite gifts that you provide." She then urges me to place the watermelon underwater at my feet. I put it where she indicates and attempt to hold it in place with my foot, but it pops up and begins to float downstream. We laugh as we watch it dance in and out of the waves. The third pregnant woman approaches and begins to chant in a language I do not understand, and then drops seven pennies at my feet. Circling around me, she pours out the liquid from the cup and says, "With these seven copper pieces I ask for your love and protection to guide our people until time's end, and may this molasses surround you with the sweet things in life."

I begin to feel dizzy once more. My eyes roll back, but I fight to stay conscious. I observe as the adults pass their flowers to the children, who then place them in the stream. Various people holding flower necklaces hand them to the pregnant women, who adorn me with a multitude of blossoms. The current seems to have come to a standstill, and the stream now looks like a field of wild white-and-blue flowers. The blossoms begin to flow toward me, as if guided by a magnetic force.

BANG!

A loud gunshot interrupts the ceremony, and most of the people on the shore disperse, running for cover. I rush to help the pregnant women who are scrambling to get to the other side of the river.

"What in tarnation is happening down here?" a loud voice roars over the crowd.

Tillie shrieks, "Uncle Phineas! Everything's fine! There's nothing going on here, just a . . . a ceremony . . ."

Phineas rides over to us on his horse. He has a

130

rifle resting on his shoulder and about seven men in tow, all carrying rifles and whips.

"Heathens! You're all heathens!" he yells.

Tillie closes his penner and slips it into her dress.

"Matilda, is that you?"

"Yes, sir," Tillie answers.

"Come here now!" he commands. He motions for her to stand beside his horse.

She holds her notebook behind her back and slowly approaches her fate.

He looks in my direction. "Is that your slave there in the water?"

Tillie lowers her head. "Yes, sir."

Phineas turns toward his men. "Go get her. She seems to be the culprit."

The few slaves who have lingered drop back, creating a clear path for the horses. The remaining flowers float toward me just as they did before the gunshot. I can feel my strength well up inside me.

One of the men jumps off his horse and confidently wades toward me. "Come on, nigger, your time is up."

He attempts to pull me out of the water. I grab him and throw him to the other side of the river.

The crowd cheers despite the presence of their master.

"Stop!" Phineas commands. "This must all stop! Turn yourself in, witch!"

"She is not a witch!" Tillie exclaims.

"Hush your mouth," Phineas says as he cuffs her on the back of her head.

"Turn yourself in!" he repeats.

I begin to have flashbacks to my recent beating. The pain, the horror, the hate. I cannot surrender to this man.

I stand in defiance.

The master orders another of his men to retrieve me from the river. This one, a young, wiry, hard-looking man, rides into the river on his horse, who is prancing and bucking at the excitement and chaos around him.

The man points his rifle at me and says, "You're a pretty one. Be nice and come on over here, so I don't have to hurt you."

I dip underwater, move beneath the horse, and grab one of the man's long dangling legs. I manage to yank him off and into the water as his horse scrambles to the opposite bank and gallops away. Pulling him all the way underwater, I pry his gun out of his hands and surface while keeping him pinned with my feet. I throw his gun to the strongest-looking African man still standing close by. I then heave the man I've pinned underwater up onto the shore, where he slams headfirst into a tree. He crumples to the ground as the master's men start screaming and shooting in all directions.

"Silence!" the master bellows. At the sound of

his voice, his men immediately pull themselves together, although they keep their guns leveled at the few remaining Africans. The large man to whom I threw the gun is nowhere to be seen.

Phineas then looks at me and with a furious trembling voice spits out, "Witch! Good Lord! You really are a witch! You will pay for this!"

He grabs Tillie and forces her to sit astride his horse in front of him. He holds a blade to her neck.

Even with this bold act, I can see that the blood has drained from his pale gray face. He looks up at the sky and intones, "The Lord is my shepherd. I will fear no evil, for you are with me." Staring at me without blinking, he seethes through clenched teeth, "Surrender, witch, or she will die!" The pressure of his blade has already broken Tillie's skin. He is not bluffing.

"I will come," I say clearly, and wade toward the riverbank.

As I maneuver out of the water he directs one of his men to ride up to Godmother, who is standing strong like a tree, defiant and still, rooted in her spot by the river. The man hits her in the head with the butt of his rifle, and Phineas screams, "Let her be the example!"

She falls to the ground, unconscious.

He motions for his men to surround the remaining Africans and commands, "Take them all back to their quarters. We'll deal with them later."

The man I threw across the river has returned to his senses, and to his feet. He is eager for revenge. He grabs my hands, pulls them behind my back, and violently ties a rope around my wrists. He tightens it until blood seeps from beneath the thickly braided twine. I show no emotion.

I steal a glance at Tillie. Her body is stiff and Phineas still has the blade to her neck.

As the man drags me along, he shouts, "Keep your eyes to the ground, witch!"

I lower my head, but the water that still clings to me from the damp dress keeps the feeling of strength surging through my body, and I have to use all my willpower to refrain from breaking the rope that binds my wrists. I fight back fantasies of wrapping the rope around the man's neck and dragging him back into the river. I could easily crush each of these men, but not before the master could run his sharp knife across Tillie's neck and end it all.

10

WITCH

"If you even think of pulling a stunt like you did at the river," Phineas threatens, "Tillie is dead."

We return to the house, and the men hold me steady, close to a heavy wooden stake planted in the middle of the grassy yard. Though my body surges with power, I dare not flex a muscle. I'm passive as the men wrench my arms back to keep me still.

The other goons are holding torches, and I wonder if they're planning to burn me alive. I feel strangely calm as I look toward Tillie's dark bedroom window. It reflects the flickering flames of the torches, and I think I can see Tillie's fragile, pale face pressed against the glass. Suddenly she's gone.

Three men pull out a dilapidated contraption from the storage house. It's a large T-shaped wooden device on a rolling platform with a chair hanging from one end and a long rope from the other. Dense cobwebs cling to it.

"Do you know what this is?" Phineas asks with a slight smile. "It's an antique I had shipped from Salem several years ago. It was used during the witch trials. I think it's high time I put this little beauty to good use." He rubs his hands the same way Tillie does when she's excited. "This here is a dunking chair," he says as he points to the contraption. "I'm a law-abiding citizen, and I would never induce a punishment without a trial." He pauses. "So, this is your trial."

He pats the device as if it were an obedient dog. I know that this man is planning something horrific, but I cannot understand his logic.

"I've done my homework on this, and it's called trial by ordeal. God shall determine your guilt or your innocence. Hell, this chair might be your best friend."

He smiles, and once again he rubs his hands together. "You see, our little dunking chair will let me know if you're guilty when we submerge you in the river. If you float up, well, that means you are a witch, and we have to execute you. And if you sink, well, I guess you're innocent."

Water? He's threatening me with water! I have to suppress a smile as I hang my head and quietly thank the irony.

"Oh, don't worry your pretty little head. I'm sure you'll prove to be innocent." Phineas cackles and his men join in. "Take her to the stables and secure her for the night," he commands. "We'll commence in the morning."

Phineas grabs my neck and looks straight into my eyes. His jaw is clenched, and a large vein is raised on his forehead. The force of his grip could kill me on the spot. I cough and he loosens his hold.

"I do not want to ruin my chance of finally using this chair." He slowly glides his hands down my back. "It's too bad. You're one fine nigger."

I hold my breath until he finally walks away.

The man from the river grabs my wrists and shoves me to the ground. I pull away and stare into his eyes. Clearly still afraid of me, he stutters, "Th-the master says to take you to the stables. I'm sure you know the way. I'll just follow you."

I begin walking down the path toward the stables. Tillie had pointed them out to me earlier. As I make my way through a cluster of apple trees in the backyard, I check to see if my shadow man is still following me. He is.

"It's just there, to your right," the man says.

The smell of the stables is particularly strong tonight, but I welcome the stench, knowing that the night will give me time to plan. The man shows me to an empty stall. As I enter, he pushes me down again, and I land on my knees in a pile of dirty straw. He binds my wrists together with more scratchy twine, reinforcing the knots that are already there. Then he threads the other end of the rope through a thick metal loop screwed securely into the side of the stall. I scoot back toward the wall and prop myself up so my arms aren't extended painfully above my head. The man looks at me and winks before disappearing into the darkness.

The dirty hay on the cold dirt floor does not provide much comfort. I can hear the horses pacing back and forth in their stalls. Their snorts and low whinnies soothe my ragged nerves and lull me into a semiexhausted sleep.

"Yemaya," someone whispers, startling me awake.

I do not answer.

"Yemaya," Tillie hisses.

"What are you doing here?" I demand.

"Shhhhhh," she cautions as she enters with a large plate hidden under a fancy silver cover.

"You really want to get yourself killed?"

Tillie's neck is bandaged and her eyes look completely swollen. I imagine she did her fair share of crying after our ordeal. She places the food on a bare patch of dirt and unties my rope from the hook. I stretch forward and roll my neck in a circle.

"Are you hurt?" she asks.

I shake my head and attempt a smile. I know that my wounds pale in comparison to the nasty cut on her throat.

She passes me a plate full of food. I grab the cornbread and declare, "Your uncle is brutal."

"I told you so, but he surprised even me

138

tonight." Touching her bandaged neck, she says, "When Auntie Soph saw what he'd done, she was appalled!"

I reach for the chicken and murmur, "I can imagine."

"My uncle threatened to kill me and my aunt if I fraternize with the slaves again. She wants me to run away with her tomorrow night. But I won't go; I won't leave you. He'll have to drown me along with you!"

Tillie starts crying, then sputters between sobs, "He's a monster. He said he'd kill all the slave children if I help you run away."

"What?"

"He's covering every possibility."

"What's your aunt doing to plan your escape?"

Tillie says with teary determination, "I'm not going. She wants us to take the same route as the slaves on the Underground Railroad."

"Tillie, you have to go with Auntie Soph. I'm going to be all right." I move in closer and whisper, "I'm going to be fine. And he will not kill the children, they are worth too much. Please concentrate on your plan to escape, and do not worry about me."

She looks at me and wipes her tears. "But the chair; you'll drown."

"I can handle the chair. I can't be drowned. It's impossible. Water is like air to me."

I can see Tillie's face register shock, even in the

139

darkness of the stable. She says, "Really? Truly? You swear on Obatala's life?"

"Yes, I swear on Obatala's life that the dunking chair cannot kill me."

Tillie suppresses a squeal and hugs me so tightly it hurts. "I'll come get you tomorrow after dark. He plans to leave your body in the river for a few days to set an example for the slaves. You'll come with me and my aunt!"

I pull myself out of her grip and touch her bandaged neck. "Can I see your wound?"

Tillie lowers her head and reaches behind her neck to untie the bandage. As she removes the beige cloth, blood and pus stick to the interior lining. The cut is deeper than I'd thought.

"It's not so bad," Tillie assures me when she sees my reaction.

I hold back my emotion. "Come."

I motion for her to lean in closer to me. I raise my wounded wrists to her neck and begin the process of healing. Tiny webs weave into braids around my cuts. After sealing my wounds, the fibers reach toward Tillie's neck. They begin to fuse with her skin. The webs cover her neck along the edges of the wound. The silken threads seal her open gash, and she coughs as the healing webs flash a glow of amber light. Her eyes show terror mixed with trust.

"Just a few more seconds," I say, with my wrist still attached to her neck.

I can feel my energy drain into her system. Her skin is less complicated than mine, so the process is simple. As I reach to wipe the webs off her neck, she jumps back.

"It won't hurt," I assure her.

I reach up again and remove the silken threads from her neck. As they fall to the ground, they reveal her perfectly healed skin. There is no scar to remind her of this nightmare. She reaches up and slowly runs her fingers across the invisible gash. Tears well up in her eyes.

"Thank you," she whispers.

I pick up the ropes and hand them to her. I turn around and slowly, she begins to retie them around my wrists. "I'm so sorry."

Tillie ties the twine with enough space for me to set myself free.

"Can you do me a favor?" I ask.

"Anything."

"Tomorrow, when your uncle is dunking me, do not cry."

She nods, scoops up the dinner plate, kisses me on the cheek, and runs off into the night.

11

REDEMPTION

The trial is set to happen just after noon. There is a crowd of white people, including women and children, waiting by the river. The master must have spread the word of my dunking.

I'm led to the river by one of the master's men, the main overseer. The crowd taunts me with both words and trash alike. A watermelon rind hits my head and falls in the dirt. I shake off the juices, and the overseer kicks me to the ground.

"Witch! Witch! Witch!" the crowd chants.

The overseer drags me to the chair. He secures me and a bag of rocks to the device by wrapping a rope around my lap and the chair. His hot breath wafts past my nostrils as he ties the burlap bag full of stones securely to the bottom of the seat. I try not to vomit from the smell. He wraps the heavy twine around me, the chair, and the stones. "Well, I guess this will make you innocent." He smiles. "You won't be floating to the top."

Beyond the sea of white faces, I see the Africans congregate. They're all wearing white and blue. *My colors!* I am grateful for this silent show of solidarity. An apple core strikes my head as the young white children continue to yell profanities.

"Order!" a voice bellows from a distance. "Order in the court."

Phineas walks through the crowd with Tillie on one side and his wife on the other.

"As many of you know, this woman here," he says, pointing at me, "has been accused of witchcraft!"

The crowd hisses and heckles.

"Order! Order!" Phineas repeats. "This here is a trial to determine her guilt . . . or innocence. Most of you know how this works, but I'll explain just in case it's slipped your mind. The witch will be dunked in the river and given a chance to confess. If the witch fails to confess, we will let the good Lord determine her fate. When we dunk her again, if she floats to the top, she is guilty and will be punished by death. If she stays on the bottom, she is innocent."

Tillie looks at me with a stone face. She still has the bloody rag around her neck to avoid suspicion. I lower my gaze so her uncle does not catch our subtle communication.

"Let's get on with it!" he commands.

Three men roll the chair to the edge of the river. I hang over the water about seven feet from the shore. The men take hold of the rope from the opposite side of the T. I dip slightly into the river until they steady their grip. I can feel the strength return to my body, but I have to exercise restraint.

Phineas stands on the bank of the river and asks me, "Do you confess to the accusations of witchcraft?"

I am silent.

"Dunk her!" he orders.

The three men release the rope and dunk me into the river. The gently flowing water surrounds me with feelings of longing for my home, for my family. On the opposite bank, wedged in a cluster of rocks, is the small watermelon from last night's ceremony. I suppress my desire to reach for it as I feel the chair lift me out of the water.

I choke and cough up water to make the onlookers, Phineas in particular, believe that I am drowning.

"What say you now, wench? Do you confess?" he bellows.

I remain silent. Before he dunks me again, I steal a glance at Tillie. Just as she promised, she is not crying. I smile to myself as I'm submerged again. The chair settles at the bottom of the river. I imagine that the master is concocting some story about my innocence because I have yet to float to the top.

I blow bubbles up to the surface, faking my death. My woolly hair flows back and forth with the current of the river. Just then a small school of little shimmering silver beauties swim by me, brushing against my body with their smooth, tiny tails. I almost laugh, imagining what it would be like to once more feel my own tail! But I remember that I have to remain still. The fish circle back and surround me for a moment. It's almost like they know I'm one of them.

I resist the urge to look up into the faces I know are now peering into the river. I float, head down, determined to stay still until Tillie returns after dark to get me.

Night seems to take forever to fall. I grip the sides of the chair and easily crush the moist wood into a splintery pulp. I must contain my emotions to avoid destroying the entire contraption before nightfall. The temperature begins to drop as the sun sets. Fortunately, I am accustomed to frigid waters.

As soon as darkness turns the river into a womb, I see a vision of Obatala as a boy. This time he is not cutting me out of a fishing net but instead breaking the ropes that bind my hands and hold me to the chair. He frees me. My wrists have been rubbed raw by the once-unyielding knots. I look at the surface and see a blurry image of Tillie squinting at me. I swim to the riverbank and pull myself out. Tillie suppresses a shriek of delight, and we embrace, cradling each other for a long time.

"Look!" She pulls away and waves a small

145

piece of paper before my eyes. "Look what I found in my uncle's library!"

My freedom certificate!

"I searched for hours after that dreadful dunking." She passes me the paper.

"I can't believe you found it!"

"*Asé*," a voice says from behind the bushes.

Seven Africans emerge, including the wild-haired man who led us to the ceremony last night.

"We are coming with you," he says.

Tillie looks up, startled and confused. The group waits in the distance as I speak to her.

I shrug and say, "We are in this together."

Slightly panicked, Tillie says, "I have to get my aunt. Follow the North Star and head up the river. We'll meet you where the river splits. We'll be there in an hour's time."

"Be careful," I plead.

Tillie looks at me, smirks, and says, "When am I not careful?"

We smile. I know that Tillie can take care of herself. She runs off toward the house.

The man who led us last night walks up to me and shakes my hand. "I do not believe we have formally met. I am Frederick. We don't have time to explain everything now, but I already have a plan. I know where we're going." I smile at him and nod my approval.

He hands me a small bundle of clothing and says, "Here are some dry clothes for you to wear on the journey." Without thinking, I pull the soaking-wet dress over my head, drop it to the ground, and stand naked before him. He looks utterly shocked, so I pull the underclothes on quickly and step into the dress.

"Frederick, can you gather everyone who is coming with us? We must leave right away."

He nods and turns to the others. I search for a secure place to put my freedom certificate. The medicine pouch around my neck seems like the best bet. I fold the paper into a small rectangle and slip it in the leather bag. I look up to see a woman with an infant tied to her back with a wine-colored wrap. She is the first to approach me after Frederick briefs them on our plan.

"I am Sadie. Godmother told me to let you know that she must stay with the rest of the slaves. She also wants you to know that you have brought her the salvation she prayed for. I am her daughter, and this is her grandson, Mayan." She caresses her son's back as she says his name.

"I'm glad to hear that your mother has survived. How did she know that I had not drowned?"

"Because you are Yemaya, the Goddess of the Sea."

Next, a young girl who looks to be the same age as Ozata runs up and almost shouts, "Yemaya." She hugs me and says, "I'm Emily."

I hug this charming, energetic child back, and I remember my love for Ozata. I realize that

Tillie's aunt probably renamed most of the slaves.

Margaret, who is standing near Sadie, says, "Miss Yemaya, I would never miss the opportunity to be your disciple."

"Margaret, I'm happy you're here."

As if on cue, three men march over to me. Although their ages vary, they are all in top physical condition. The eldest speaks first. "We've been sent to protect you on this journey. The man over yonder is Frederick."

"Yes," I say, nodding, "we met."

"He's very intelligent. He reads and makes smart decisions. This here is Crooks," he says, pointing to the man in the middle. I recognize him as the brawny man I threw the gun to. "He is our strongest hand. Not much going on upstairs, but he has a mighty muscle."

Crooks takes a step forward and says, "Don't listen to him, I'm fine in my brain." He pulls the gun from behind his back and shows it to me with a proud smile.

The youngest of the three men introduces himself. "*Asé*, Yemaya, I am Clementine. Samuel's firstborn."

Clementine is clad in trousers, a button-up shirt, and boots. I thought she was one of the men. Her mannerisms match those of her male counterparts.

"*Asé*," I respond, and turn to her father. "So, you must be Samuel."

"I am, but I think we best be on our way."

"What will happen to the others we leave behind?" I ask.

"They have made their choice to stay. May we be in God's favor, and they as well. At least the master believes you're dead."

Frederick leads the group through the dense forest next to the river to keep us hidden. The wolf and the owl create an eerie melody over the steady rhythm of the crickets and bullfrogs. The forest seems to come alive during the hours of darkness.

Young Emily grips my hand as we forge forward. She is obviously scared. We are in danger, but I squeeze her hand and whisper, "Don't be afraid, I'm here with you."

"Will they send the dogs?" she whispers back.

"Yes," Frederick quietly retorts, "so keep your voice down."

"Dogs?" I question.

"Yes," he repeats. "We'll have to walk in the river so they can't track us. We should go now." He ushers our small group to the river. Emily hesitates as she dips her foot in the water.

"You'll be fine," I assure her as I pick her up and carry her in.

She wraps her short legs around my waist and her skinny arms clasp my neck. "Are there any monsters in the river?"

"None in the river," I insist.

I hold her tight as we continue upstream. As usual, the water has imbued me with strength enough to carry all of our group. I can hear the river swelling in the distance. I pass Emily to Crooks and walk up to Frederick.

"I am going to swim ahead to check out that noise."

"I'll come with you."

"No, stay here with the rest. They need you."

He would surely slow me down. I dive in and forge forward. The current quickens as I approach the source of the sound. I rush past a blur of rocks and water plants and leave behind a tunnel of minuscule bubbles as I speed ahead, undaunted by the current's resistance. Two different temperatures of water seem to mingle here. I raise my head above water and spot where the river splits up ahead.

"Yes!" I say aloud.

I swim back to let the others know that we've nearly reached our rendezvous point.

"What was it?" Frederick asks.

"It's where the river splits," I eagerly respond.

"Let's get there, then," Frederick commands with enthusiasm. "We will take the right fork, to the north, to get to our first stop before daybreak."

Emily's teeth chatter in the frigid air. Although I can move freely, the others are struggling against the growing current and the dropping temperature.

"How much longer?" Emily asks.

I take her back from Crooks and hold her on my shoulders above the water. The night air is humid and warm compared to the river. Emily should fare better up there. The others trudge forward without complaint.

Frederick turns toward me and asks, "About how far up was the split?"

"We should be there soon."

After about a mile of pressing through the current, we reach the split.

"I think we're safe to stop and wait for Tillie on the other side of the river," I say. "Everyone seems to be cold."

"Tillie?" he asks.

"Yes, she and her aunt are meeting us here. They'll travel with us. They'll be here soon."

Frederick nods. I can see his uncertainty, but he doesn't question me.

We climb onto the marshy banks of the river. It is nearly a new moon, so the thin crescent provides a minimal amount of light. Our eyes have adjusted to the night, and I can see that there are no large or threatening animals nearby.

"I guess we just wait," Samuel says.

"Let's hide in that grove of trees over there until they arrive," Frederick says.

We each find a spot to rest, except for Emily, who skips around as everyone reminds her to quiet down.

Branches crackle and everyone freezes. Emily whispers loudly, "It's a dog!"

"Shhhh," Frederick commands as a lone coyote pokes its nose into the grove of trees. He sniffs, freezes, and lopes back the way he came. Emily giggles as the rest of us exhale with relief.

"Hey, Emily," Frederick whispers, "have you ever heard about the people who could fly?"

Emily's eyes light up. "No!"

"If you keep your voice down," Frederick explains, "I'll tell you the tale."

Frederick commands the attention of the entire group. When he speaks, people listen. Sadie unties the scarf from around her back and begins to breastfeed her child. The boy has been so quiet that I almost forgot he's with us.

Frederick begins:

Once, in a land far, far away, there lived a tribe of people who could fly. They were a proud and magical group. They had invisible wings that enabled their miraculous feat. Nobody doubted magic in their tribe, so they were free to explore the supernatural. One fateful day, these mystical people were taken away from their motherland and forced onto slave ships. The crew that enslaved them could not see the tribe's invisible wings, so when they packed them into the ships, they jammed them so tight that all of the people lost their wings. That was only the beginning of their misery.

Once they arrived in the new land, they were taken to a plantation. They worked alongside other slaves who knew nothing of their magic. It almost seemed as if the tribe had forgotten who they really were. One day, a young woman, exhausted from the day's work, asked the medicine woman of the tribe to use her magic to grow back their wings. The medicine woman said, "We have toiled long enough. It is time to return to our magic, our life force." As she conjured her ancient magic, she and the other tribespeople sprouted their wings and soared away from the plantation. The other slaves watched in awe. They passed the story of the people who could fly down through the generations.

Emily yawns. "Could the people really fly?"

"That's what they say," Frederick says, smiling.

Although the story is meant for Emily, we know that Frederick wanted to share it with us, too.

"It's been well over an hour," Clementine says in a nervous tone.

"I am aware of that," I say, searching for any sign of Tillie.

"We will have to get moving again soon," Samuel adds. "The night is our cover."

Where is she?

"We can set off in ten minutes," I say.

I pass Emily to Margaret and walk toward the stream. Something must be amiss. Tillie should have been here a while ago. The night is quiet, too quiet. It feels like the calm before the storm.

I hear footsteps in the distance across the river. I squint my eyes. Suddenly I hear a bark. The dogs have arrived! I rush back to the group. "They'll be here soon! We must move!"

I grab Emily and turn to run upstream.

"Wait!" Frederick commands. "We won't get far if the dogs are already here. You take the group up the right fork of the river, and I'll run on foot up the banks of the left side. The dogs will follow my scent."

We are all silent.

"There is no time to hesitate; you must hurry. If you stay the course, by daybreak you'll find a cave where you can hide. A man will meet you there tomorrow night; he'll lead you to the next safe place." Frederick is about to continue with his directions when the barking is suddenly a great deal closer.

"No," Margaret cries, "we must stick together."

Frederick has no time to respond. He takes off and races along the bank of the left fork.

I gather everyone else. We run to the water and

plunge in. Frederick is well out of sight, but we can hear the dogs in pursuit. Instinctively, we fall into a train-like formation, holding one another's waists. I lead us toward the right fork. The current is strong, so I tell Sadie, who is gripping my waist, "Hold on tight. Pass the message back."

She quietly delivers the message down the line as we fight the force of the river, trudging upstream. Emily is clinging to me as she did before. We take the right fork, and the waters become easier to navigate. We wade silently along.

12

THE FAMILIAR

We walk and wade and trudge, pushing past our limits multiple times throughout the night. But, sure enough, just as the rising sun threatens to expose us, I see the cave Frederick told us about up ahead, near the riverbank.

"We can rest here for the day," I say as I lead the group out of the water.

We crawl up the steep bank, slippery with wet rocks and moss. I hold Sadie's hand to help her up the hill. The cave sits at the entrance to the forest. I usher the group in before I enter with Emily, who is asleep with her head on my shoulder. As I sit down, she mumbles, "Where's Frederick?"

"Hush, child," I answer. "Go to sleep."

She drifts back into her dreams. I am in no shape to explain our loss. I have sacrificed too much. I've lost my parents, my home, my beautiful tail, Richard, Tillie, Frederick, and maybe even Obatala. *Will we ever hold each other again? Is he still alive?* I make a promise to myself that everyone with me now will arrive at our destination. I cannot bear another loss.

Crooks volunteers to stand guard for the day.

"Are you not tired?" I ask.

"I don't need much sleep, ma'am."

I marvel at the strength and courage of my small crew. I'm beyond exhausted and finally succumb to sleep, feeling safe for the first time in many days.

When I awaken to the brilliant morning sunshine a few hours later, I realize that this cave is the one Ozata and I shared weeks ago. There are small carvings on the wall that she made while we were here. I touch the medicine pouch around my neck. Miraculously, it is still intact.

Everyone is asleep, so I tiptoe to the mouth of the cave, where I see Crooks leaning against the wall.

"Ain't no trouble following us, I can tell you that. Or else they would've been here by now."

"Why don't you get some sleep, then," I suggest. "I'll keep an eye out."

"Thank you, ma'am," he says as he bends to enter the cave.

I walk over to a large boulder. I recognize it, and I trace the jagged edge I'd crumbled when I was here with Ozata. I hold the pouch again, seeking the wisdom of Cora's tribe. I hear her whisper in my ear, *Follow the path of the familiar.*

"What does that mean?" I question aloud.

The chirping birds are the only answers I

hear. Splashes of water from the river sprinkle my face. I hold my pouch in my hand and head down to the water. There is a flat rock that bids me welcome, with a perfect place on it to sit. I wash my face in the river and regain my strength.

The others sleep for most of the day. The water has taken a toll on their systems. Sadie's infant wakes up for his feeding and falls straight back to sleep. As they awaken, I tell them about Richard and that his house is a stop on the Underground Railroad. Although they are hesitant to show their excitement, they share a look of relief.

"I'm hungry," Emily complains.

"I know, dear," I say to comfort her. "There will be plenty of food tonight."

Clementine pulls out an apple from her bag. "Here, eat this."

Emily jumps up and grabs the sweet fruit. "My favorite!"

"My tree bore fruit for the first time only days before we left. I have more we can share." She pulls out three more apples and passes them around. Each person takes a bite and gives the succulent fruit to the next person. Inexplicably, the apples satisfy our hunger.

Margaret even stops before the apple is finished. "I am full, thank you."

Emily stares at me. "What do you think happened to Frederick?"

I scan the faces of our group, but they stare back, waiting to hear my answer.

"I'm sure he escaped."

Emily jumps for joy. "I knew it! I knew it!"

The others are silent.

Samuel walks to the mouth of the cave and checks out the surrounding scene. "The sun is starting to set. We should get our things together, so we're ready to go when the man comes to get us."

I walk over and join him.

"God protect us," he prays as he turns toward me.

The night air is crisp. Thankfully, we do not have to travel by water tonight. The group would not be able to withstand the chill of the river.

"I'm ready," Emily says, grabbing my hand.

As the sun sinks and the forest disappears in the darkness, we decide to walk toward Richard's house, rather than wait for the man Fredrick told us about here. I can't help but wonder what Sara will say.

We fall into our previous formation and walk out of the cave in a single file. I lead the group through the forest. We pass a split tree that I remember seeing when Richard was carrying me in his arms. I am reassured that we are going in the right direction. We should be close to the main road soon. I turn to check on my group. They appear well rested and ready for the journey. Crooks brings up the back of the line, and his muscles seem to pulsate with each step he takes, daring any danger to confront us.

Margaret walks deep in silent prayer or contemplation. The men are scattered throughout the line. Sadie cradles her son close to her bosom. As usual, Mayan is quiet and content.

We walk toward the main road, careful to stay in the thick of the trees. As we approach the dusty path, I veer right to continue in the direction of Richard's estate. Lightning bugs dart around us, as if the stars have descended to guide us.

Emily jumps to catch the fiery flies. She is intrigued by their glowing tails. They remind me of shimmering jellyfish surrounded by their halos of light as they bob and dance in the depths of the sea. Emily pulls me out of my reverie by reaching for my hand.

"Where's your ma?" she asks.

"My mother is in heaven."

Emily bows her head. "I'm sorry."

"Have I not told you of my journey?"

"No," Emily says with excited expectation.

"I left my life and all that I knew in the waters that kiss the western coast of a great and faraway land called Africa."

"Oh! Is that where the people who can fly are from?"

"Yes, and it is also where your ancestors are from."

Emily giggles and skips close beside me, leaning in to hear my whispered tale.

"I left the ocean because I fell in love with a fisherman. He was gentle and strong all at the same time. I followed him to this new world."

"Is he Obatala?" Emily asks.

I freeze as she utters his name. "Yes, Obatala. Do you know him?"

Emily smiles coyly and sings, "No, but I know you and Obatala have many children."

"I have never had a child."

"Well then," she says as she crosses her arms, "you just haven't reached that part of the story yet."

We hear galloping horses approaching in the distance. Emily and I drop down as I signal the rest of the group to lower themselves and hide in the brush. As the horses near our location, Sadie's baby begins to wail. She attempts to calm him, but the damage has already been done.

The lead rider stops his horse just ahead of us. He tries to peer through the dense foliage, and even though he cannot see us, Mayan has already given us away. The rider steers the horse into the forest. The beating of my heart seems louder than the boy's screams. Every bone in my body wants to run, but I cannot leave anyone behind.

"Yemaya? Yemaya?" the rider shouts as he slides off his horse. "It's me, Richard."

I stand up, surrendering to his protection. "You

found us," I whisper with relief. "How did you know it was me?"

He looks at the others, who are all slowly standing. "I was looking for you. Didn't Frederick tell you?"

"He didn't have a chance. He said a man would meet us at the cave, and I thought it might be you, but I wasn't sure."

"Where is he?"

"We heard dogs, and he ran away from us to make them follow his scent instead of ours."

Richard nods gravely and says, "He's very smart. I imagine he figured out how to evade them. The entire county is looking for you. There is a sketch in the paper of you. They are offering a hefty reward. It says you are an African witch."

He pauses, awaiting some reaction, but we remain silent.

"Come," he continues, "I will explain more when we get to the house."

We follow him to the carriage. Richard instructs us all to climb inside. We have to sit on the floor and on top of one another.

"I'm sorry it's so cramped, but it won't be long, and we can't afford for any of you to be seen."

There are four other men with Richard. His butler drives the carriage, and three others are on horses. One of them leads the pack, and the other two protect us from behind.

We arrive at Richard's estate within minutes.

His butler opens the carriage door and we practically tumble out before he can help us. Richard takes my arm and leads me across the lawn toward his house as the others follow behind.

"Is Sara here?" I whisper in his ear.

"No. I sent her up north."

A sense of relief settles throughout my body. We walk to the back of the house.

"I prepared a space in the cellar for you. I don't want to take any chances. Everyone is looking for you," Richard emphasizes.

The butler lifts the cellar door open to reveal a staircase obscured by darkness. He grabs his lantern and balances it over the opening. The light flickers, creating the illusion of dancing shadows on the walls. Unbroken cobwebs frame the doorway. I walk toward the stairs with Richard.

"It won't be like your last room, but it will do. I'll have the cook prepare some meals."

"Thank you, Richard."

We all duck to avoid the sticky cobwebs as we follow the butler down the stairs.

I glance back at Richard. The punishment for hiding runaway slaves must be severe. He is risking his life for us.

The cellar is cold and damp, and the moisture in the air is thick, infusing my body with strength.

"It's scary in here," Emily says, breaking the silence.

Richard crouches down to her level and says sweetly, "I'll bring lanterns full of oil for you. You are safe here." He stands, faces me, and says, "We will plan your next move once you get some rest."

The floors are lined with mattresses.

"I didn't know how many people were with you. I wanted to make sure you were comfortable."

Emily jumps on the mattress that is illuminated by the glow of the lantern. "This is my bed!"

The others place their belongings on the various mattresses throughout the room as Richard and his men disappear into the darkness.

13

A NEW DAY

I awake to the sound of a rooster crowing. The rising sun peeks through the small, high windows. Pink-and-yellow hues melt together in the sky. I hear Sadie's son suckling on her breast as she slumbers. The others are still fast asleep. Specks of dust float in the sun's rays.

Emily seems smaller as she sleeps, curled in my arms. The sunlight reaches her face and her eyelids begin to flutter.

"Good morning," she whispers.

I rub the top of her head. "Good morning, angel."

Our dishes from last night are spread out around the room. I begin to gather them quietly and stack them by the stairs. Emily helps by collecting the water glasses.

"Richard is nice," Emily says as she places the glasses by the stairs.

"Yes," I say, "he is very special."

"He's white and nice, like Tillie."

I giggle a little. "Yes, he is."

My smile fades as I wonder why Tillie and her aunt never made it to the river. I hope that they escaped from the house and are heading north.

We hear the creak of the cellar door opening. Emily jumps and runs behind me. A voice calls from the top of the stairs, "It's just me."

Richard arrives at the bottom of the stairs, followed by his butler and a woman. The servants collect the dishes and leave. Richard has a large wicker basket full of fruit that he offers to us. Emily dives for a red apple, then runs straight to Clementine and jumps on her mattress, shrieking, "Look! Look!"

Clementine is startled awake but calms down when she sees Emily's smiling face.

"They are just like your apples!" Emily says as she passes the juicy fruit to her.

"Is this for me?" Clementine asks.

Emily nods and runs back to Richard.

"You want another?" Richard laughs.

"Please."

Richard picks out the largest apple and hands it to her. Emily takes it back to her bed and nibbles on it. She is content for the moment.

Clementine walks over to Richard and says, "I'm Clementine."

Richard responds with a firm handshake and says, "Richard."

"Thank you for this," Clementine says with deep sincerity.

"It's good for now," Richard says, "but we have to figure out a plan to move you to the next station."

Clementine nods in agreement.

"When the others wake up we'll discuss our plan." Richard gestures toward the back of the cellar and says, "That's a false wall. There's a small opening over there, down low. It's concealed, but when you pull the cover off, it's big enough for a man to fit through. If you have to hide, you'll need to crawl through the opening to get behind the wall."

Clementine walks to the wall and inspects the covered entrance.

Richard looks at me with such warmth that I'm taken aback.

"Is everything all right?" Richard asks.

"Yes, it's just . . ." I falter. "I don't know— you're doing so much for us."

"May I say something to you in private?"

"Yes, of course."

He takes me to the small hallway that leads to our makeshift privy.

"I've thought of you every day since we first met," he confesses as he takes my hand. "You can't go with the others. You're in too much danger. If you stay with me for a few days, I'll be able to make sure your journey north will be safe . . . or safer."

"But I can't," I blurt out.

"Just think about it. The others are at more risk with you around," he says as he moves toward the stairs.

I sit in the hallway to sort out my thoughts in private, but Samuel walks toward me and says, "I don't mean to bother you, but . . ." He points to the small room behind me with the rusted bucket that Richard set up as our outhouse.

"Of course!" I respond as I jump up from where I am sitting. "Sorry."

I rush past him and make my way back to the mattresses. The others are roaming about the room, peeking out of windows and investigating the space.

"How long do you think we'll be here?" Margaret asks.

I conceal my emotions and answer her with a steady voice. "Richard will be back soon to discuss the plan."

"I'm feeling a bit scared."

"I would be worried if you weren't," I say with a smile.

"I've been praying for Tillie."

"Me too," I answer. "Me too."

The four walls seem to close in on me as I try to conceal my tears. Crooks stands at a window, tapping on the frame. Sadie and Margaret croon over baby Mayan just two beds down, and Clementine shows Emily how to play a game with her fingers. I am surrounded by stimulation, noises . . . people. I cannot hide—or think.

Samuel returns from the hallway. "You look like a horse trampled you," he says rather loudly.

The entire room falls silent and stares at me. Once again I attempt to lie, but the words will not form. "I'll be fine" is all I can say.

The women and Emily slowly gravitate toward me. Sadie hands me her baby. "He's really good at making people feel better."

Mayan smiles as I settle him on my lap. He is a plump child, and his wide eyes stare at me as if he can see straight through my soul. The chaos inside me begins to subside. I can feel his innocence and smell his sweet baby scent. The child begins to laugh as I bounce him on my knee.

"Silence!" Crooks demands as he peers out of a window.

The child is the first one to respond to Crooks's command. His smile fades, and Sadie swoops down, takes him from me, and cradles him to her bosom.

"Quickly!" Clementine waves her hands toward the wall. "Stack the beds and head to the wall space."

We gather our belongings as Clementine and the men quickly stack the mattresses against the wall. She leads us to the corner of the room. There is a small opening at the base of the wall. Sadie hands her baby to me as she crawls in first. I pass her the child and then usher Emily through the opening. We all huddle in the tiny space. Just as Samuel covers the opening behind him, we hear loud pounding on the cellar door. The lock gives way and a torrent of footsteps pound down the stairs. Emily squeezes my arm.

"This is private property!" Richard yells.

"We're the law, son," one man proclaims. "Kindly move out of our way."

"There's nothing here, sir," another man says, about two feet from our hiding space.

"Why do you have these beds?" the first man asks.

Richard explains, "These are my slave quarters. I insist that they keep it clean and stack the beds every morning."

Another man must have made his way to the indoor privy. "There is fresh waste in a bucket back here!" he yells.

"You do realize the severity of harboring runaway slaves?" a man snarls.

"The waste is from *my* slaves," Richard insists.

"I'll be watching you, Richard Dillingham," the man shouts as his footsteps disappear up the stairs.

Richard must have followed them out of the cellar. The stark silence feels almost as threatening as the yelling. I can feel the sweat from Clementine's back soaking the front of my dress. We are all stacked behind the false wall. Sadie's baby grunts as she attempts to breastfeed him. Emily holds tight to my arm.

We stay in the same position for what seems

like hours. None of us dare to speak or ask any questions. My limbs have fallen asleep and are practically numb.

Finally, the cellar door swings open. Emily grabs my dead arm and pulls it toward her. We hear each step creak on the stairs. Clementine's back begins to sweat again as I hear someone walking up to our wall.

The false flap opens. "It's only me," Richard reassures us. "I am so sorry," he says as he pulls each of us out of the space.

Emily seems to be the only one not physically affected by being cramped for so long. She skips around the room as we all attempt to regain feeling in our legs.

"It is not safe for any of you here. The sheriff said that there are bounty hunters in every county searching for you. He had the poster with your face on it," Richard says as he stares at me with his crystal-blue eyes. "They're now accusing all of you of murder and witchcraft."

"Murder!" Samuel scoffs. "Who did we murder?"

"I didn't ask any questions," Richard responds.

We all quietly stand in shock.

Richard breaks the silence. "I have someone coming tonight to take you to the next safe house, but I'm afraid that I cannot, in good conscience, let Yemaya go with you. She's the only one with a bounty on her head, and the only one of you with her face plastered on every tree."

"What?" Emily gasps. "Yemaya has to stay with us!"

She looks to the others for support, but no one responds. Emily runs up to me and hugs my waist. I rub her hair and comfort her. "You'll be fine, my love."

I look at my people, drenched in sweat and shaken by fear, and assert, "I think Richard is right. You should not have to pay for this."

Margaret walks up to me. "This is not your fault."

"Thank you, Margaret, but you should travel together up north. I will meet you there."

I hug Emily tight to me and add, "I promise."

14

ALONE AGAIN

The Underground Railroad guides come for everyone else from my group late in the evening. Richard's staff has prepared food for the journey. Richard hands a musket to Crooks, who still has the rifle I threw to him. Crooks shows Richard the gun and is about to hand the musket back to him when Margaret intercepts it.

She says, more forcefully than I think she means to, "Give me that!" She grabs it and then shrinks back a bit, and adds more softly, "Thank you. I'm a good shot." She smiles and marches up the stairs to join the guides.

My stomach drops as I watch them disappear into the dense forest. Richard takes my hand and says, "They'll be all right. I have my best men protecting them. Come with me. I have an attic space that may be a better fit for you. I want you to get your rest." He leads me to the main house, ushers me to the top floor and down a long hallway. There is a trapdoor in the ceiling that he pulls down with a long metal hook.

"I'll bring a lantern for you."

His blue eyes meet mine, and he whispers,

"I don't even know who you are. Witchcraft?"

"Do you actually believe them?"

"I'm confused," he admits.

Smiling, I take his hand and squeeze it. His cheeks turn red, then he nods and says, "I have a friend visiting who I want you to meet. Can I bring him to the attic in the morning?"

"Yes."

I am oddly comforted by my solitude in the tiny attic space. The quiet reminds me of my life in the ocean. I always felt connected with everything around me, at one with the sea and all those creatures who shared it with me. The noise of this human world on land is often jarring and overwhelming. These humans never stop talking. The Mer don't chatter simply to fill up space.

The morning sun glistens through a small window in the attic ceiling. The air at the top of the house is crisp, in total contrast to the basement's dampness. Although the lack of humidity weakens me, my lungs appreciate the fresh air.

My mind drifts, and I think of Sadie, the baby, Margaret, Emily, Clementine, Crooks, and Samuel. They had become my family in the few days we spent together. My heart tightens as I wonder if I'll ever see Tillie or Frederick again.

And then there is Obatala. I feel too much pain to even think about him. Nevertheless, as soon as he enters my mind, I am consumed with thoughts of him. My pulse begins to quicken as my breath deepens. A tingle in my lower belly intensifies with each breath I take. As I reach to massage the sensation, I hear the scratch of the long hook on the attic door.

As the trapdoor creaks open, I hear Richard yell up to me, "Good morning, Yemaya!"

I lean over the opening and see him standing below with a silver tray full of food. A sickly-looking white man is with him.

Richard nods at his friend and says, "I've brought my good friend Waldo to join us."

Richard hands Waldo the tray of food and places a long ladder at the opening to the attic. He takes the tray back and sends Waldo up the ladder, then follows him.

The two men sit beside me, and I cannot help but notice Waldo's poor state of health.

"You are not well," I observe.

Waldo looks at Richard. "She cuts right down to the truth. My kind of lady." His charisma seeps through his sickened pores.

"I brought Waldo to meet you because the two of you are—how can I say this?" Richard pauses. "Unique."

I look at Waldo; he is surveying me.

"Waldo, did you bring that piece you read to me a few years back? The one I love?"

Waldo pats his pocket. "It's with me at all times."

"Will you give us the honor of reading a section of it?" Richard inquires.

Waldo clears his throat. "I don't want to be a bore."

"Nonsense," Richard interjects. "We would be honored to hear your writing."

Waldo pulls a brown leather journal from his pocket, and, handling it as if it were his freedom paper, he says, "Here is a little section; it's entitled 'The Over-Soul.' "

He repositions himself as he begins to read. " 'We live in succession, in division, in parts, in particles. Meantime within man is the soul of the whole; the wise silence; the universal beauty, to which every part and particle is equally related, the eternal ONE.' "

I am speechless. This stranger understands me!

Waldo closes his journal and looks to me for a reaction.

"I . . ." I falter as I attempt to respond. "I have never heard words that so perfectly describe how I feel."

Richard smiles. I can tell he is pleased that I understand Waldo's genius.

"Are you saying that we're all connected?" I ask Waldo.

"Well, the parts are seen from a fragmented perception. Meanwhile, the soul can only be one."

"So, we are everything? The sun, the moon,

the animals, the trees all look as though they are separate, but they are . . . we are really all parts of the whole. The soul?"

"Brilliant!" Waldo says, grabbing a penner from his pocket.

He begins to scribble wildly in his journal. I look at Richard and shrug.

"I got it!" Waldo exclaims. "Have a listen: 'And this deep power in which we exist and whose beatitude is all accessible to us, is not only self-sufficing and perfect in every hour, but the act of seeing and the thing seen, the seer and the spectacle, the subject, and the object, are one. We see the world piece by piece, as the sun, the moon, the animal, the tree; but the whole, of which these are shining parts, is the soul.' "

"Did you just write that?" I ask.

"Why, yes." He smiles. "Inspired by you, of course."

"Why are you letting yourself die?"

"Pardon me?" Waldo says with a touch of shock in his voice.

"You have a great understanding of life's principles, but you are not putting them to use."

Waldo becomes a bit uncomfortable.

Richard attempts to bail him out. "Maybe we should have our tea?"

"No, Richard," Waldo assures him. "I have been running long enough. Can I share something with you, Yemaya?"

I nod.

"Long ago, the love of my life, my late wife, Ellen, died of consumption." He pauses and holds back his emotions. "She was my everything. I lived and breathed for her. I put all of my love into her. So, when I buried her in the ground, much of my life seemed to be buried with her. I even tried to dig her up to see if I could find that missing piece."

I can see his shame as he confides in us. "Nothing was there but a rotten piece of meat. That is what I have become," he says as he lowers his head. "A rotten piece of meat. I can't even be there for my current wife. She has been so understanding, but I know she deserves better."

"May I?" I ask as I move forward to touch him.

I place my hands on the back of his neck. Richard does not see the webs as they fuse into the pores on Waldo's back. His cells are weak and depleted. My webs find the source of his disease and glow while they remove it. I collapse to the floor in exhaustion.

Richard reaches for me. "Yemaya!"

"I'm fine," I whisper.

Waldo looks at his hands and his arms. Viewing his now plump, vibrant body, he asks, "How did you do that?"

I smile faintly. "It's just as Richard said: we are both unique."

Richard stares at Waldo's face, visibly stunned.

178

He turns to me and asks, "What just happened?"

I lie on the floor for the remainder of our conversation. I can tell that Richard is concerned for me. Waldo, on the other hand, seems to know that I'll be fine.

"I have been coming down from the North every year since my sickness appeared, in hopes that the good weather would help. I don't remember ever feeling this alive." Waldo seems delighted as he reaches for a plate of food.

Richard rubs my shoulder. As he does so, some of my strength returns.

"Do you want to sit up?" Richard asks with great compassion.

I do not feel the need to sit, but I know that doing so will bring Richard peace of mind. He helps me up and leans me back against one of the short attic walls.

"Can I get you something to eat?" he asks.

"Some of that tea will do fine."

Meanwhile, I look at Waldo. He is greatly enjoying his meal. Noticing me observing him, he says, "Please excuse my vigor in eating. I do not mean to seem uncompassionate about the state of your health, but this meal is the first one that I have truly enjoyed in years."

Richard pours a cup of tea and hands it to me. As I sip the tea, my body extracts the water and regains more of its strength. I quickly crawl toward the food tray and grab the kettle. Instead of taking the time to pour myself another cup, and then another, and so on, I drink straight from the pitcher, downing the tea in one enormous swallow.

The two men stare at me in silence.

I look at the empty jug and ask Richard, "Did you want some?"

They laugh as I place it back on the tray.

"At least it wasn't too hot," I say in between my giggles.

"I feel like I have found my people," Waldo exclaims.

"A runaway slave, a privileged abolitionist, and a hopeless philosopher," Richard says with a hint of irony.

"That should be the title of your next book," I say as we all laugh.

The pyramid-shaped space of the attic is full of joy and laughter. Waldo has healed me with his words, and I have returned his favor.

"How long are you staying here?" I ask Waldo.

"I leave at the top of the week. In three days' time."

I hold his hands in mine. "You must promise to visit me each day and read to me from your journal."

Richard clears his throat. "We will all leave in three days. I have another mission in Tennessee and Waldo must head back to Boston. I have made a plan for your journey up north as well.

You will be pleased to know that Ozata and her mother will harbor you for two days."

I am pleased, but then I remember. "I thought it was dangerous for me there."

"They have established themselves in the tribe," Richard explains. "Ozata has made a place there for a stop on the Underground Railroad. For some reason, the tribesmen who would usually be disagreeable to such an idea have turned a blind eye toward her."

"Ozata did this?"

"With her mother's help."

I turn to Waldo. "I suppose I will be leaving in three days' time as well."

He smiles. "In the meantime, I promise to read to you."

15

THREE DAYS

I find myself awaiting Richard and Waldo's return. I have occupied myself with dressing in the new outfit Richard left me last night. I'm grateful for the new boots and good, heavy coat. But the day is long, and there are no windows in my reach to see outside. I can feel the sunlight through the ceiling window, but as the hours pass, I forget about the sun's warmth.

I hear the familiar scratch of the hook on the attic door. The flap swings open and Richard makes his way up.

"Where's your friend?" I ask.

"He went for a walk in the woods. He is thrilled about his new lease on life."

A buzz of mild excitement takes hold of me as Richard settles down. He looks at me and says without reservation, "I am always taken aback by your beauty."

I blush and lower my head.

"You do know how beautiful you are, right?" he asks.

He takes my hand and kisses it.

"Stay with me for a while," I suggest.

We lie on the wooden planks and stare up at the sun's rays. I hold his hand and listen to his musings.

"I can die now," he says.

"Why do you say that?"

"It's just a saying. It means that I have reached my happiest point, and I would be ready to die."

"You will live a long life."

Just then, Waldo briskly climbs up the ladder to the attic.

"The weather is quite fine for early October." Waldo smiles. "As a matter of fact, I have never experienced weather as nice as today's."

He sits down, claps his hands, and rubs them together. He glances at Richard, then blurts out, "I know I'm not supposed to say anything, but don't pay any attention to the folks who are accusing you of witchcraft."

I look at Richard.

"I had to tell him," he admits.

Waldo continues, "You are like Jesus Christ himself." He seems to be drunk with joy at having been healed. "But let us not speak of religion, nor politics, for that matter."

Richard finds humor in Waldo's comment.

"I want to speak of the beauty in the world. I can finally see and feel all of the concepts that my mind has been trying to tell me for years. I am at one with the honeybee collecting pollen from the flower. I feel it."

I take this moment to express my doubts. "Sometimes I feel the connection, and other times I feel so alone."

"How we *feel* changes nothing about the fact that we are all one. Whether we know it or not, the universal intelligence still assumes its role in connecting everything as the Eternal One. Our best bet during those times of doubt is to rely upon faith. Faith that one day we will see the light again."

Richard chimes in, "We Quakers call that God. Quakers believe that God is in all of us, that we each have the ability to access God directly. We do not have to go through an intermediary, like a priest or a minister."

I experience a deep urge to reveal my true identity to them. They engage in conversation as I contemplate whether or not to tell my secret. The reality of my existence is far beyond any concept they have discussed. *Will they be afraid of me if I tell them everything? Will they believe me? Will they think I'm really a witch?*

"I'm not human" spills from my mouth before I can stop myself.

They stare at me with absolute confusion.

Waldo breaks the silence. "I feel that way sometimes."

I remember Richard putting a folding knife in his breast pocket earlier. I reach over and grab it from him. The men freeze in fear. I open the knife and cut my leg.

"No!" Richard yells.

I motion for him to keep back. The wound burns as the blood begins to pour out. I close my eyes and summon my healing powers. The blood stops as the weblike fibers begin to weave around the wound. The webs glow, and my skin tightens as the tiny threads pull the gash closed.

When the process is done, I gently wipe the blood and fibers away to reveal my perfectly healed skin.

The men are speechless, much like I felt after I heard Waldo's words.

"Witchcraft?" Richard whispers.

I shake my head no.

Waldo reaches over and touches my leg. "Why, I have never . . ."

I hold his hand.

"Is this what you did for me?"

"Yes."

"We have just borne witness to a miracle!"

Richard is still processing the experience. He picks up his pocketknife and examines the blood. He wipes it off with his handkerchief and places the knife back in his pocket. Meanwhile, Waldo stares at me with wide eyes.

"You said that you are not human. I have, for a long time, suspected that there are other forms of life among us. May I be so bold as to ask . . . what are you?"

A loud noise startles us.

"What was that?" Waldo yells.

"Pick me up," Richard commands him.

Waldo interlaces his fingers and Richard steps into the foothold he has created. Waldo hoists him up to the attic window. Richard peers out and then punches the attic wall. "Those bastards!" he yells.

Waldo drops him down. "What happened?"

"The men from town set fire to the stables! You stay up here," he says to me, and the two of them fly down the ladder and disappear through the hallway. In their haste, they forget to close the attic door. Richard left a pitcher of water last night. I pour the water over my head, pull on my coat, and climb down the ladder.

The water seeps through my pores and imbues me with strength. I run through the dining room and peek out the window. Five men on horseback are scattered about the yard.

Richard is in the stable setting his horses free. I cannot find Waldo.

"What are you doing down here?" a voice asks from behind me.

I turn and see Waldo loading a rifle under the arch of the dining room ceiling.

"I have to help," I say.

"Come this way."

We sneak to the front of the house, walk outside, and stand on the top step of Richard's front porch. Waldo raises the rifle toward the sky and shoots into the air. I jump and hide behind the porch fence.

"I'm trying not to bring attention to myself!"

"Sorry," Waldo says as he walks straight toward the men and shoots at the ground by their horses' feet. Two men are bucked off as the others congregate around him.

"Now!" Waldo yells.

Richard's staff run out from behind the house and startle the rest of the men. The invaders pull the horseless men onto their remaining steeds and ride off of Richard's property. The staff races to the stables and begins to douse the fire with water from a nearby pump.

My hair is dripping wet as I peek through the porch fence.

"Guess they didn't need me," I say aloud, smiling to myself.

Richard storms by and walks directly into the house. He slowly steps back and looks straight at me. "Why are you down here?"

"I thought I could help."

"Come on," he says, motioning for Waldo and me to follow him into his study. "We need to get you out of here now. They're going to bring the rest of their boys from town back here. Ozata isn't expecting you until Sunday, but we have to send you now. Did you leave anything in the attic?"

I feel for my pouch around my neck. It is still there. "No."

"I'll pack you some food and a blanket. You have to go now!"

He pulls a copper box out of the bottom drawer of his desk. A ringing tone resounds throughout the study as he slams the box on the table. He pulls a chain necklace with a key from around his neck. He unlocks the box and grabs a handful of golden coins.

"Do you have someplace to keep this?" he asks.

I shake my head no.

Richard rummages through the drawers and finds a small leather pouch. He places the money in the bag. "Do not let anyone see this. They'll think that you stole it. This is ten times your bounty, enough to buy you a hefty plot of land. I cannot stress to you enough to keep this hidden. No Negroes—hell, no white men—are running around with this amount of gold on them. Use this to buy any goods you need. Do you understand?"

I nod, although I don't really follow.

"Promise me you will keep it hidden."

Waldo leans in. "How much is that?"

Richard shoots him a look.

Waldo smiles and says, "Hey, I've been your friend for quite a while now and I've never received such a gift."

I am inspired by Waldo's ability to remain lighthearted with so much chaos around him. Richard pats him on the back and says, "If we survive this, I'll share my estate with you."

"Let's put that in writing." They both laugh.

Richard hands me the bag, and I gently tuck it in the inside pocket of my coat. He reminds me again, "Keep it hidden."

We run to the kitchen, and Richard prepares a small bag of bread, fruit, and salted dried meat. He fills a leather canteen with water and hangs it around my neck.

"Now!" he urges as he shepherds me to the door. "Let's go!"

I trip onto the porch. When I catch my footing, Richard is standing in front of me. He grabs my shoulders and says, "I will never forget you."

I caress his face. No words form over the lump in my throat as Richard kisses me—first on my hand, then my cheek, then my forehead.

Waldo smiles. "Get going!"

I give Waldo a huge hug, and I run off the porch.

"Follow the river north," Richard yells, "upstream!"

I turn for my final farewell. Richard and Waldo wave from the porch as I realize that I never got to tell them who I am.

16

RIVER RUN

The river welcomes my return with a sharp swell. The deeper water has quickened the current. I am tempted to jump in and swim upstream, but I opt to simply splash myself with the water and run on land. Although the money is securely hidden inside my coat in a tight leather bag, the food will surely be ruined in the river.

I duck beneath tree limbs as I race through the forest. I forgot to ask Richard how far I'm traveling. He seemed to think that I could make it there in one day. Thoughts of Waldo's philosophy race through my mind as my momentum increases. I feel as though I am running on air, with no resistance or fatigue. I'm suddenly hit with a sharp pang against my chest. I trip on the forest floor, tumble to the ground, and pass out.

As I come to, I see that several Native warriors have surrounded me. They speak in an unfamiliar tongue while keeping their bows and arrows trained on me. One of the men approaches me and removes an arrow that had been meant to strike my heart. It lodged in the small wooden

Mer figurine tucked inside the pouch Ozata made for me instead. The approaching warrior inspects my chest. There is no wound.

Slowly, he holds the pouch up and shows it to the other men.

They lower their weapons and inspect me. The leader says something to the rest, and they cautiously move in and surround me. One man helps me up, and they guide me through the forest, away from the river.

As we enter a village, I realize that this must be the nation that Richard described. They are a much larger tribe than Cora's community. Hundreds of people seem to roam about the village doing their daily chores. Women carry water in clay pitchers, weave pictures into ornate blankets and shawls, and cook in front of their homes. The men sharpen spearheads, build animal traps, and work on their houses. The people of the tribe pause and stare at us as the warriors escort me through the village. Children gather around like ants circling a piece of fruit.

A large round home, about twice the size of Cora's, stands in the center of the village. The men walk me to the birchbark structure. The lead warrior enters first.

Several minutes pass before I am allowed to go in. A man who is more ornately dressed than any of Cora's people sits with a woman on the floor.

He wears a hat full of feathers and several vibrant necklaces. Upon his chest rests a decorative armor of sorts composed of long white beads. He is most definitely the chief. There is a large parchment with several symbols written on it between him and the woman. The chief motions for me to sit with them.

"I am told you have a medicine pouch from one of our sister nations. Can you understand what I am saying to you?" he asks in Cora's language.

"Yes."

"Good." He smiles. "Because my guest here despises English."

The woman, clad in a colorful robe, spits on the ground.

"Why are you here?" the chief asks. "Are you a runaway slave?"

I pause for a moment, not sure what to say. "I'm a free Negro," I say, indicating the pouch around my neck. "My papers are here."

I open my pouch and begin to pull out my freedom certificate. He stops me.

"That won't be necessary," he says as he passes a pipe to the woman.

"I am here to see Amitola. She was rescued from the raid."

"This is why you speak their language. Yes, she and her family are here."

"What is your name?" the woman asks.

"I am called Yemaya."

"I am Ayoka. I am visiting to teach the children of this tribe how to read and write," she says as she passes me the pipe. "You are welcome among my people. Our nation is west of here."

I take a puff from the pipe and begin to cough. The two of them laugh at me. As I compose myself, I notice the parchment again, and say, "If you don't mind my asking, what is this? Some of the letters I recognize, but there are plenty that are new to me."

"Do you know how to read?" Ayoka asks.

"Yes," I answer, "in English."

"These are the symbols in our language."

The chief, who seems uninterested in my conversation with Ayoka, looks at me gravely and says, "I cannot guarantee your safety here. We're dreading the threat of removal, and some of my people return slaves for rewards."

"Removal?"

"*Nunna-da-ul-tsun-yi.* The Trail of Tears," he translates.

"I don't understand."

"The white men are forcing our people to leave their land and move west. I will have my men take you to Amitola." He then sends me out without giving me a chance to say a proper goodbye to Ayoka. The warriors silently escort me across the village.

Ozata is the first to notice my arrival and shouts with glee, "Yemaya!" I break away from the warriors, run to her, pick her up in my arms, and swing her around.

"You're here early!" she exclaims. "Is Richard well?"

I smile and deflect the question, asking, "Is Cora or your mother here?"

Ozata knows I'm concealing something from her, but she doesn't push me. She grabs my hand and leads me to her house.

"They will be here soon," she says as she indicates that I should sit down with her outside while we wait for them. I remove my food sack, and Ozata reaches over to inspect the puncture in the leather pouch around my neck.

"What happened?"

"I was struck by an arrow coming here."

"They meant to do that. If they'd wanted to kill you, you'd be dead. I'll make you a new one." She ducks into her home and fetches a circular piece of leather. She presents it to me and proudly declares, "This is buffalo skin—powerful medicine. Your old one is deerskin—gentle medicine, but still strong. It's a reminder to be kind."

"My kindness was shot."

Ozata laughs as she places the leather on a rock. She picks up two other rocks. One is long and sharp, and the other is flat. She punches holes along the edge of the leather by placing the sharp rock on the buffalo hide and hitting it with the

194

flat one. As she finishes the last hole, she picks it up and holds it up to the sun.

"Perfect." She grabs a black leather string and skillfully weaves the cord through the holes in the hide. As she pulls it through the final hole, she tightens the ends to form the pouch.

"Done!" she says, dangling it in front of my face. "Let's put your medicine inside."

I remove the old pouch from around my neck and hand it to Ozata. She carefully pulls out the amulets from the pouch: the Mer carving, the arrowhead, crumbled sage, and finally my freedom certificate.

"What's this?" she asks as she wipes the sage pieces from it.

"It is the form that proves I am a free Negro."

"Oh," she says, carefully placing it into the new pouch. She then holds up a fresh sprig of sage, inserts it into the pouch, and ties the cord around my neck.

"The buffalo hide will protect you and give you strength and power. How does it feel?"

I hold the pouch in my hands and feel its energy surging through my body.

"It feels very powerful. I love it! Thank you."

"We must bury the old medicine bag by a tree, so that the energy can go back to Mother Earth."

There are numerous trees surrounding the perimeter of their land.

"That one," I say, pointing to the largest one in the area.

"Interesting. It's not always wise to be the largest tree. We must know how to bend and compromise, like the willow, or else we will go down with the storm."

"Are there any willows?"

"No," Ozata says with a big smile.

I point to a smaller tree. "Then that tree will do." We laugh.

We walk to the tree and dig a small hole. Ozata hands me my old pouch and says, "You must do it."

I kneel on the damp earth and gently place the medicine bag in the soil. I scoop the dirt into the hole, pack it tightly, and smooth the spot.

Ozata closes her eyes and says a special prayer:

> O, Great Spirit, who is in everything we touch and everything we see, hear us as we return to you your medicine. Make our hearts open to your beauty. Make us wise so that we may follow your voice. We pray that when it is time for us to return to the earth, we may be held in your arms once more.

As we open our eyes, we see Ozata's mother, Amitola, standing before us. "You are early," she says with a smile. "Ozata, will you gather berries for tonight?"

"Yes," Ozata says as she skips away.

Amitola turns to me and asks, "What happened?"

"The townsmen came and set Richard's stables on fire—"

She interrupts, "The horses!"

"They are alive. Richard saved them."

"And Richard?"

"He was fine when I left, but he seems to think that the men will return."

"Did they see you?"

"No."

"You were not followed?"

"No."

"I ask because we are with a hidden sect of this nation. The government is trying to send all of the tribes out west. They've sent many of our people there."

"The Trail of Tears?"

"Yes," she says with surprise. "You've heard of it?"

"The chief mentioned it."

"Oh, Great Spirit! He knows you are here!"

"Yes, I met with him, Ayoka, and a group of warriors."

"You met Ayoka?"

"Yes. The warriors captured me and delivered me to the chief. He gave me permission to stay, but he could not guarantee my safety. Ayoka was with him."

"Interesting," Amitola says. "I wonder why he took a liking to you."

"I think it's because we were speaking in your tongue."

Amitola nods her head and agrees, "Yes, that would do it."

"Ayoka doesn't live here?"

"She is from just west of here—Tennessee. She comes here to teach us how to read and write in this nation's language. She has promised to teach Ozata."

"Yes, she had a parchment with the symbols."

Amitola stacks wood in front of her home.

"I cannot stay long. Richard gave me the directions to the next stop on the Underground Railroad." I want to tell her about the bounty on my head, but I have a sense that she knows.

"You may choose to go, but know that you are welcome here," Amitola reminds me.

"Thank you, but I think it would be wise to leave in the morning. I will take this day to rest. Is Cora around?"

"Yes, she has been waiting and praying for you. As soon as she found out that you were coming, she began planning a celebration. She will be pleased that you arrived early. We will have a feast tonight to bless your departure."

Ozata comes running back with a basket full of berries.

"Thank you," Amitola says.

Panting, Ozata asks, "Are we doing the shake dance tonight?"

"Yes," Amitola responds as she walks inside with the fruit.

I wait for Ozata to explain the shake dance, but she proceeds to stack the rest of the wood in front of the firepit.

"What is the shake dance?"

"Did we not do it with you before?"

"No."

Ozata sets the wood down, sits beside me, and explains, "The ancients say that as we move through the day, many things stick to us: bad moods, sickness, jealousy, fear, pain." She leans in toward me. "They stay with us unless we let them go with help from Great Spirit. As you dance, the bad feelings shake off and return to Mother Earth, where they can be cleansed and used for good."

Later that night, the survivors of Amitola's tribe gather for the ceremony. They take turns blessing me with prayers and well wishes. Cora stays by my side while Ozata paints my face with two white lines across my cheek. Others around me have painted faces and are dressed in ceremonial garb; the men are in deerskin breechcloths, and the women are wearing colorful ribbon skirts with blouses that leave one shoulder bare. Some are wrapped in vibrant wool shawls that whip around their bodies as they dance.

The drummers beat out complex rhythms as the tribe fans into a large circle. The women and children move to the center and Cora leads me into the group. Everyone begins to jump up and shake. I follow their lead. We dance for several minutes. I look to Amitola, hoping for a break, to rest. She motions for me to continue, so I bounce to the tempo. After some time passes, my vision blurs and my mind is transported back home.

As the bubbles clear, a tail fin flaps a wave of water in my face. I am swimming with my parents again. My mother smiles and my father hands me a small oyster shell lined with mother-of-pearl. It is the shell he was holding in my last vision, but this time he gives it to me. He squeezes my hand to reassure me, and the vision fades away.

I return to the shake dance, jumping up and down and shaking vigorously. I realize my hand is clenching something. I slowly open my palm to reveal a beautiful shiny oyster shell. I quickly slip it into my medicine bag. I've learned not to question the powerful magic of this tribe, but this is difficult to comprehend. Did my father somehow just give me this shell?

I shake my head in disbelief as we switch positions with the men. The tempo of the drums accelerates and they jump, keeping their arms straight down by their sides as they dance. As if on cue, they all begin to stomp on the earth and sing up toward the heavens. The women and children hold hands around them. There are significantly more women than men. We encircle them, leaving plenty of room for the men to dance.

BANG!

The white man's weapon can be heard over the drums.

Everyone falls silent as the chief of the tribe walks into the middle of the circle. One of his warriors secures the musket in a belt around his leather skirt.

"I do not like to be disrespected!" the chief shouts for all to hear.

Everyone seems to be holding their breath.

He holds up a large poster with a picture of me on it and a caption that reads:

WANTED ALIVE
AFRICAN WITCH
REWARD $300

He looks me dead in the eye and bellows, "You told me you were a free Negro!"

I dig through my medicine pouch and pull out my freedom certificate.

He walks up to me with his entourage following close behind. "What do you have to say for yourself?"

"I am free," I say as I hand him my certificate.

He grabs it and rips it to shreds. "Many people could use a bounty like this, including me. I have never seen such a handsome sum for an African witch."

A whisper crawls from my mouth: "Can we speak in private?"

"Why should we not tie you up here and now?"

I speak in the few words of his language that I picked up during the day. "Please, and may Great Spirit bless you."

He doesn't trust me, I can see it in his eyes, but he is intrigued by me. As I speak to him in his language, he softens.

"Come, let us talk." He motions for me to follow.

"I have an offering for you. I must get it from the house."

"Very well," he says, and he sends one of his warriors to follow me.

I run into Amitola's house and grab my leather purse. I pull out a handful of gold pieces. It looks as if Richard has put quite a few coins in the pouch. I have no time to count it now. I hide the pouch under some clothes and run out.

The warrior stops me and pats me down. As soon as he determines that I carry no weapon, he sends me off to the chief.

"Please take this as an offering for sparing my life," I plead as I pour the coins in his hands. "It's twice the bounty."

He holds the money up and asks, "Did you steal this?"

"No. That is the truth."

"You must leave at dawn, and never come back."

I bow as I back away. "Thank you." I turn and run toward my people.

Cora, Amitola, and Ozata stand anxiously awaiting my return. Amitola whispers, "He let you go?"

"Yes. But I must leave now. Too many know of the bounty."

They lead me back to the house, where I quickly gather my belongings. As I reach for my leather purse, I notice that Ozata is silently crying in the corner.

"Ozata," I whisper.

"I will never see you again," she says.

I embrace her, knowing that her prediction is most likely true. "You will always be in my heart."

Ozata reaches up and catches one of my tears. She wipes it on her medicine bag. "The tears of a mermaid are powerful medicine."

I try to hand Cora some coins from my leather purse.

"No!" she adamantly refuses. "This is too much."

"Richard gave me more, and I want to share it with you," I insist. "Put it aside for an emergency. Maybe the tribe can use it to buy land."

"Land can never be bought," she says as she lowers her gaze.

Cora reluctantly takes the money. I tuck the purse into my clothing and hurry out the door. Ozata and Amitola follow me to the edge of the forest. I have learned to appreciate quick farewells.

"Where will you go?" Amitola inquires.

"Richard told me of the next safe house on the Underground Railroad. I will find solace there on my way north." I hold Amitola's hand as I attempt to convince us both of my safety.

"May the Great Spirit bless you," Ozata says.

Amitola nods in agreement and says, "Be safe."

"Thank you," I say. We all embrace one another.

As I begin to run through the forest, I hear Ozata yell, "Are you going north to find Obatala?"

I smile as I'm reminded of my love. "Yes!"

17

NORTHWARD BOUND

Once again, I'm swimming toward an unknown destination. I see the waxing crescent of the moon as I peer up through the river water. The night is dark without the light of the full moon. I speed through the waters, refreshed and renewed. The current is high, so I have to barrel along at full force. I can make it through the night, but come morning I will have to find something to eat.

Suddenly, I slam into a huge object. Stunned, I lift my head above water to see that it is actually a large man. He remains crouching in the water with a look of terror on his face. He is at the end of a long line of frightened African people, all crouching and silent. A woman in the front of the line holds her finger up to her lips, begging for my silence. I hear the faint sound of dogs barking in the distance. The woman motions for the people, maybe as many as eight, to duck farther into the river. We all kneel, careful not to make a sound. Our heads are just barely above water as we hear the barking gradually ebb into silence.

"Come," the woman whispers as we slowly stand to follow her up the river through the black of night. The man I collided with remains on his knees. I walk around him to join the rest of the group, but the woman is still bending over and trying not to speak above a whisper.

"Come," the woman urges again, "we must hurry."

The man refuses to move and just stares ahead as if he doesn't hear her.

"Come," she repeats with more intensity.

"This will never work," the man whispers in a trembling voice. "I have to go back."

The woman, who I see is quite tiny when she stands up, splashes quickly downriver to stand in front of him. She pulls a revolver from a pouch she has tucked into her belt and hisses, "You go on, or die!"

Visibly shaken, the man staggers to his feet and splashes past me, continuing to journey forward.

As she wades by me without acknowledging my presence, the petite brown woman mutters, "I haven't lost a passenger yet."

She seems confident that I will follow her, so I make my way to the back of the line and trudge slowly against the current with the group. No one questions my presence, perhaps because any noise, including the sound of our voices, is a threat to our safety. Although I could easily bypass this crowd and continue underwater, something tells me we are headed for the same safe house. The woman leading the group holds up her hand, motioning for us to stop. She points up toward the riverbank, where a large tree with drooping limbs caresses the surface of the river.

"This is it. Run," she commands.

Like day-old molasses, the river slows the group's movement. They attempt to rush from her waters, only to realize that the way to make progress is with measured, deliberate steps. The harder they flail, the more cumbersome the water becomes. My body is still infused with strength from the river water, so I must restrain myself from bypassing the crowd.

As we come out of the water, we gather by the tree trunk before being instructed by the woman to follow her, single file, through the forest. The soft stampede of human feet on the forest floor is almost too eerie. We are running for our lives.

Up in the distance, I see a lamp flame flickering off and on.

"Follow the light," the woman commands.

I sprint swiftly and silently, my movements effortless as I anticipate refuge, food, and sleep. The night is particularly cold. While it does not bother me, I imagine that the others are not comfortable. The group is breathless as we finally make it to a log cabin tucked away in the forest. A white man with a long gray beard stands tall, holding the oil lamp high. His breath forms billows of smoke in the frigid night air.

"There's the Quaker," the woman says as she leads us to the light.

He ushers us around back to a secret opening leading to a basement.

Our weight upon the planks of the rickety makeshift staircase seems to threaten their stability, yet no one takes caution to move slowly. As we rush down into the basement, the woman stands at the opening and talks with the bearded man. Still no one has questioned me. The whites of their eyes seem to glow with anxiety and fear. The bearded man hands the woman his oil lamp as she walks down into the space that we will call home for the night.

"Don't think I haven't noticed you," the woman says as she pats down the dirt beside me. She holds her skirt to the side, sits down, and declares, "They call me Moses."

"Yemaya," I respond.

"Oh, I know who you are. You may be the only Negro woman they want more than me," she says with a sly smile. "As you have probably guessed, we are headed north."

"How far are you going?"

"To Canada. You'll come with us. It's not safe for runaways anywhere below the border."

"I'm going to New York. Cicero, New York."

Moses gives me a strange look, nods, and then draws in a deep breath and releases a soulful hymn. The others, while folding their clothes and readying themselves for sleep, quietly sing along. The spiritual becomes my lullaby and allows me to drift peacefully into slumber.

The next morning I awaken to a spider crawling on my hand. Its furry legs carefully scale up my arm. It is surprisingly similar to the crabs I used to watch with fascination back home.

A shiny, weathered hand gently removes the spider and places it on the dirt floor. Moses sits beside me again and says, "You will soon see that I am a woman of few words, but I have been guided by a vision to let you know this."

She holds her head as if she is in pain, then takes a deep breath. I sit up and listen intently.

Moses pulls out a tattered piece of parchment and says, "Obatala wrote this for you."

My heart trips over itself and beads of sweat shoot through my pores. Before I can ask her about my love, she recites it, barely looking at the words:

> You love me the way
> Water loves the earth.
> Soil, seeds,
> Flowers, trees.
> Pouring forth life.
> Raining down love,
> Gathering in sparkling, crystal drops of light.
> You love me the way water loves me.

I remember once
The water of your love
Became something more . . .
It was a part of all the water there is.
And I had to look away from you
Because in that moment,
I spied the other half of myself.

She stares at me. I am unable to speak, completely wrapped up in the tapestry of my love's words.

Moses explains, "Obatala was on my last mission. I was debating with myself about whether or not to tell you, because love can make one too emotional to depend upon in our situation. A woman transcribed it for him while a fellow tribesman translated it from his native tongue. I memorized it, but I took the parchment to give to you. I knew we would meet."

He does love me. The angelfish flutter in my stomach again—they have always been right.

"He loves you dearly. Every move he makes is in search of you. I did succeed in convincing him to join the movement, but his priority is to find you. I'm not sure where he is now, but he gave me instructions to leave him a message at the safe house in Canada if I found you."

I want to touch her, hoping that he touched her as well, and that his essence is somehow still lingering upon her skin.

"In a vision I had last night," she says as she holds her head in pain again, "I saw that New York will not be as you hope. I pray that you come with us to Canada. You will be safe there, and perhaps Obatala will have made his way back there by the time we arrive."

"I must go to New York first. I'll join you in Canada in short order," I say with determination.

"My visions are clear and true. New York will not be good for you," she says gravely, imparting a final warning as she clings to a tattered Bible.

"I have to see to it that a friend is safe in Cicero. She is depending on me."

"I made a promise to Obatala that if I came upon you in my journeys, I would bring you to him." She takes in a deep and bitter breath as she hands me the parchment on which the poem is written. "Against my better judgment and my clear visions, I will make sure you reach New York."

The bearded Quaker man and his wife, a petite woman with a humble demeanor, bring down several bowls of soup broth. The room is quiet as we sip the surprisingly delicious liquid.

"I am Christopher," the Quaker says. "You are welcome to stay here as long as you need. The winter will be upon us soon, and I want to make sure you reach your destination before then."

"Winter is our ally," Moses says. "Everyone

keeps to their home. No one goes in search of runaways in the snow."

Christopher does not question Moses. I have observed that she is fearless and that her moves are strategic and precise. She has no patience for insecurity or uncertainty.

Christopher whispers to her, "This is a large group. Are you sure you have room for more?"

"Yes," Moses says without hesitation. "They'll be here come nightfall. I will keep the lantern on."

Christopher and his wife gather the empty bowls and head back to the main cabin. Now that we are safe, the others are becoming curious. I hear whispers from the group.

"Gossip is from the lips of the devil!" Moses says to the whispering women. "If you have a question, ask. We are all family now. We are all responsible for each other."

One of the women stands and attempts to look at me. Her eyes dart from side to side as she asks, "Is it true that you're an African witch?"

"That's nonsense," Moses cries. "We are all children of the Lord. Do not listen to the powers that want to separate us. Yemaya is a beautiful young woman."

Blood rushes to the surface of my skin. I feel exposed. The women are not convinced. They are quiet for now, in fear of Moses's wrath, but they are not satisfied.

"Do not be swayed by their petty fears. We have greater dangers to contend with," Moses says in an attempt to comfort me.

I follow her to the corner of our dirt basement and ask, "Who is it that we are waiting for?"

"You heard Christopher?"

"Yes."

"It seems as though a couple of our friends need some assistance."

"Are you sure it's fine for me to join you?"

"This mission is blessed by the Lord himself," Moses pronounces as she holds her hands up toward the sky. "There is room for every passenger because this train is bound for glory. Plus, we could always use another strong woman on our mission." Moses falls into divine rapture and saunters to the other end of the room, humming a spiritual.

The sunlight seeping through the cracks in the basement door slowly fades and the chill of the night air settles around us. The three gossiping women remain close to one another. At this point I believe they are merely sharing body heat. Although I am aware of the change in temperature, I am not bothered. In fact, the colder and darker my surroundings, the more I am reminded of my dwelling deep on the ocean floor.

I lie down on my straw mattress but am unable to sleep. My mind races, imagining Obatala reciting the poem. I pull the folded paper from my medicine pouch and reread it. My fingers outline the ink of his words and I suddenly catch a whiff of his fragrance. I breathe in the scent of my beloved and gently close my eyes. His lips curl up into a tender smile as I reach behind his neck and trace the three familiar scars with my fingertips. My body begins to tingle with an overwhelming feeling of desire. Before our lips touch, I am pulled from my fantasy by the sound of the basement doors creaking open.

We silently await our fate.

"It's me," Christopher announces, sensing our fear. "We've brought rice and broth for supper."

Four people carefully step down the fragile staircase carrying bowls of soup. I imagine it's all he and his family can afford to feed such a large group of visitors. Christopher walks up to Moses and says, "The two we were waiting for have arrived."

I'm the last one to get my food because I have claimed a space in the far corner of the room. One of the people distributing the soup makes her way toward me.

"Are you hungry?" a familiar voice asks.

I squint to see more clearly, and whisper, "Tillie?"

Startled, Tillie places the bowl and lantern on

the ground and flings herself at me. Her body is quivering with emotion as she exclaims, "My God in heaven, is it really you?"

She kisses me all over my face, then turns back toward the door and yells, "Auntie Soph! Come quickly! Yemaya is here!"

Tillie's aunt trips over someone as she hurries toward the back where I am sitting. When she sees that it is really me, she claps her hands together and says, "Oh dear! We were so worried about you."

"You know each other?" Moses asks.

Tillie stands and gives Moses a long embrace. She's the only person I've seen relate to Moses with such warmth.

"We need to get you home," Moses says to Tillie. "Your parents are worried sick."

"Will you come with me to Cicero?" Tillie asks me.

"Yes, of course. I want to make sure you get home safely. Then I'll travel to Canada to wait for Obatala."

Tillie's eyes widen, and her lips pinch into a smile. She looks at Moses and says, "You found him?"

Moses nods. Tillie grabs her shoulders and says, "Minty, do you know what this means?"

I stop Tillie and say, "Moses thinks I shouldn't go to New York at all. She had a vision that things will not go well for me there."

Tillie instantly becomes serious and asks Moses, "Is that true?"

Moses nods again.

Tillie looks at me and says in the same serious tone she's just used with Moses, "Have you heard of Minty's visions? They are accurate. Extremely accurate. You should go directly to Canada. I'll be fine. I can make it home on my own."

"Don't be silly, I'll just drop you off and then go directly to Canada."

I yearn to forget Moses's prediction, but she has infected me with a sense of doubt. Tillie simply stares at me, shaking her head. After a brief pause, she abruptly moves on to another subject.

"Did Yemaya tell you what happened at my uncle's plantation? How she narrowly escaped death?" Tillie asks Moses.

"Well, I have heard stories," Moses responds, not seeming the least bit interested.

"I first saw Yemaya when my uncle brought her home from town. She'd already been badly beaten. I had so much compassion for her, but I knew I'd be hanged if I showed it. So, I prayed she would be delivered to me. When she was close to losing her life, my uncle looked at me and said, 'Tillie, you like to take care of sick animals; take this one.' My prayers were answered. I convinced my uncle to let me put her in the guest room. There was no possible way that she would have survived out in the elements.

Yemaya was beaten so badly that her flesh was torn completely to the bone in many places. The next morning, she was fully healed!"

A loud scream from outside startles us, and we fall silent. We hear dogs growling and barking, and then, "Help! Help!"

Everyone freezes in a state of fear, but I'm up the stairs and pushing through the basement door before I can process what's happening. A pack of wolves is trying to take a young boy, one of Moses's passengers who must have snuck out when the Quakers brought us our food. The wolves, sensing my power, release the boy. I scoop him up in my arms and carry his limp body down the flimsy stairway.

With each step I take, my skin begins to sprout webs from every pore. The threads intermingle and wrap around the boy's wounds. As I enter the room, one of the three gossiping women releases a guttural moan. The boy is clearly her son.

"Take him away from her!"

"What's happening?"

"She's really a witch!"

"Someone do something!"

People are yelling, but still the child remains in my arms. We are protected and sheltered by the luminous webs that surround and heal the boy. I can feel my energy draining. I gently collapse to the floor, tethered to the boy by my silken threads. The voices are completely muted now.

They sound like a distant choir humming the spiritual that Moses shared. As we both begin to stir, the webs fall away and float gently to the floor. The boy's mother runs up to us and holds us in a tight embrace. She weeps deeply as she takes the boy from my arms. He is healed completely.

"My Lord! My God. Thank you, Yemaya," she says, weeping and holding him tightly as she leads her beloved child to the far end of the room.

Everyone in the basement has fallen silent. The only sounds are the sniffles of the boy's mother and the wood settling on the stairs. I lower my gaze, not sure what to expect next. The man I knocked over in the river stumbles to his feet and places a silver watch by my side. One of the other gossiping women walks up and drapes a knitted shawl over my shoulders. From dried fruit to family heirlooms, the people spare no expense in their gratitude.

I close my eyes to keep the tears from forming. When I open them, almost everyone in the room is staring at me in expectation. I begin handing back the gifts. I thank them all and explain that though I am deeply moved by their generosity, I cannot accept their only worldly possessions.

Moses approaches and wipes the excess webs from my skin. She whispers, "I told you we could use another strong woman on this journey."

Tillie walks up to me and sits by my side. Her aunt goes over to the far side of the room to check on the boy. We have all come together, as fellow travelers and souls. We have become the Eternal One, just as my friend Waldo spoke about. We are in this together, united by the knowledge that we need one another to survive.

18

ON THE MOVE

The Quakers secure our next stop, and we are ready to set off on our journey. Along with the boy I saved from the wolf, there is one other child traveling with us. She looks to be around two years old. Moses brings the girl's mother a glass of liquid. The mother takes in a whiff of the concoction and unintentionally contorts her face. She bribes her daughter with a piece of fruit to drink the fluid. Within minutes, the child is fast asleep in her mother's arms.

Tillie whispers to me, "She'll be fine in the morning. Minty knows all about the power of herbs. In fact, she would be considered a witch for this knowledge if she were ever found out." Tillie's whisper becomes a hiss of righteous indignation as she continues, "It's just appalling to me that whenever a woman has special abilities—or any abilities at all, for that matter— she is deemed a witch!" She explains what I've already discerned: "Minty sedates the children to keep them quiet during the journey."

"Why do you keep calling her Minty?"

"That's her nickname."

Moses walks by and tells Tillie, without making eye contact, "I changed it, dear, and you may call me Moses."

"Moses?" Tillie says, nodding her head. "Very fitting."

We say our farewells to the Quaker couple, and before we head back to the river, Moses, Tillie, Auntie Soph, Christopher and his wife, and all of Moses's passengers hold hands in a circle. Moses invites me to join them. They close their eyes and recite these words in perfect harmony: "Lord, make me an instrument of thy peace; where there is hatred, let me sow love; where there is injury, pardon; where there is doubt, faith; where there is despair, hope; where there is darkness, light; and where there is sadness, joy. In Jesus Christ's name, amen."

Tillie holds my hand as we walk toward the river. Once again, everyone is quiet. Moses turns around and whispers, "I have a few signals I use that I need to share with you."

She extends her hand straight up to the sky and says, "This means *stop*." She then closes her hand into a fist and says, "This is *silence*."

We all memorize her sign language, knowing that our lives will depend on her quiet instructions. From *dogs* to *light* and even *pray,* Moses has created a hand signal for every word or warning we will need.

The night feels calm, somehow free of our

usual anxieties. Flurries of snow lightly kiss my skin and melt into crystal droplets of water. Each drop infuses my body with strength.

"Tonight, we are untouchable," Moses says to the group. "When our faith is high, there is no man who can bring us harm. We will make it to the next stop with no interruptions."

Just as Moses predicted, we make it safely to the next house before the sun rises. The estate is sizable and well kept, much like Richard's place. We are led toward the front door by a butler holding an oil lamp. I know now that when an oil lamp flame is flickering on and off, it is silently and secretly indicating the location of a freedom house—a small but powerful beacon letting us know that safety awaits.

Tillie squeezes my hand firmly as we draw near the entrance. She smiles at me, and I understand that she is not scared but excited.

As we stand on the front porch, a young brown-skinned girl runs out of the house and shouts, "They're here!"

A white man quickly follows behind. He gently shushes her, but whispers loudly enough for us to hear, "Quiet, honey, you know the rules."

The girl looks like Sara or Margaret, the child of a white man and an African woman. Before I can make any assumptions, the white man tenderly picks her up and leads us into the house.

"Daddy, there are so many," the girl exclaims, quivering with excitement.

As we enter the foyer, a beautiful, stately woman with dark auburn-brown skin walks down the stairs. She is wearing a deep green satin dress with a loud pink sash and shiny black boots. I marvel at her confident stride, completely unhindered by the precarious-looking heels of her delicate boots. I am enchanted by her style and impressed by her air of authority.

"Mommy!" the young girl shouts as she shimmies out of her father's arms.

The woman grabs her daughter's hand, walks up to Moses, and says, "You have done well, Moses."

She goes on to greet every one of us with a loving caress on our shoulders. As she saunters my way, she squints.

"Yes, Lorna Mae," Moses says. "It's her."

Lorna pulls me into a powerful embrace. I feel a tinge of awkwardness.

We follow Lorna down a wide hallway decorated with paintings and lavish chandeliers. She ushers us toward a large hardwood wall in the back of the house. The father slides the wall to the side to reveal a substantial hidden space. There are chairs, tables, and even beds—a far cry from our last refuge. The mother of the young girl in our group places the sleeping baby, who is a picture of pure peace, on one of the many beds.

The house staff lay out plates of chicken, mashed potatoes, greens, cornbread, and tea. I'm starving, but I wait until everyone has a plate before I allow myself to indulge. Tillie brings me an embroidered napkin to place on my lap as we eat. Lorna motions for the butler to close the sliding wall. She and her family stay and dine with us.

Lorna walks up to me and says, "Forgive me for not introducing myself. I am Lorna Mae. This is my husband, Jozef, and our daughter, Tela."

Tela runs up to me and shouts, "Are you the African witch from the poster?"

"We have all heard about your story of escaping death and slavery. You have become an underground hero."

"I'm no hero," I insist.

Little Tela sits in my lap and caresses my face as if she can't believe that I'm real.

"Our heroes are the ones who do not let anything get in the way of freedom . . . of love . . . of humanity," Lorna relays with passion. "To us you are a hero."

She reaches over and tenderly removes Tela from my lap. "They have to get some rest now," she tells her daughter. "They have been up all night."

Lorna carries Tela to the corner of the wall. Jozef follows.

She slips her fingers into a discreet slot and

unhooks a lever, allowing the wall to slide open.

"Sweet dreams," Lorna says before Jozef slides the wall closed.

We turn down the oil lamps and begin to drift off to sleep. There are no windows or doors, so the darkness is intense. There are only the faintest flames still burning low to keep the lamps on. I can see only silhouettes when usually I can identify every object in the faintest moonlight. As I lie awake in the dark, I think about how Lorna called me a hero. I don't think I'm a hero; I'm just using the powers I have to survive. Moses has devoted her life completely to the service of others. She is the true hero. The line between waking and dream life blurs, and I finally fall asleep.

As I stir awake, the room is still in total darkness. I have no idea of the time. My head sinks into my pillow as I turn toward the sliding wood wall. My thighs brush together, and I feel a slick wetness between my legs. Did I urinate in the cot? I feel around for an oil lamp and turn up the flame. I'm bleeding!

Startled, I attempt to send my healing webs to the wound, but they will not activate. My panic escalates sharply as I realize that I'm not able to heal myself. The blood continues to drip down my legs.

"Tillie, wake up," I whisper, my voice shaking

with fear. "I'm bleeding between my legs."

A hand grabs my shoulder, and I jerk away.

"It's just me," Moses says.

"I cannot heal myself. Something's wrong. I'm bleeding . . ." I pull up my dress and show Moses where the blood is coming from.

Moses gently pulls my dress back down and says in a soothing tone, "You're fine, my child. It's just your cycle."

"My cycle?"

"Your menstrual cycle, your moon. That is why your webs will not activate. You are not wounded." She continues, a rare touch of concern in her voice, "Dear child, is this your first time?"

"Yes."

Moses folds a blanket and places it on the cot. "We can wash it out tomorrow. Sit."

I sit on the folded blanket. My stomach is lurching powerfully. I am downright uncomfortable. Suddenly Moses takes my chin in her hand and makes piercing eye contact as she says, "You are a woman now, for your cycle allows you to bring forth life."

Moses returns to her cot and I settle in under my sheets. I am startled by her words. *A woman now? Does this mean I can have babies?* Despite my discomfort, I think fondly of all the beautiful children who have accompanied me along my journey. My stomach cramps, and I bow to the pain and fold my body protectively around my belly. I drift to sleep, envisioning myself carrying Obatala's child.

I awake several hours later. A heavy cloud of fatigue surrounds me. I attempt to get up, but the majority of my senses simply want to return to sleep. Moses spots me as I stir. She brings over a folded rag and says, "Lorna brought this for you. She will be back shortly to take you inside the house for a bath. The rag goes inside your undergarment to catch the blood."

The latch from the sliding wall clicks and Lorna stands at the opening with a crisp, folded white towel. She is clad in a flowing silk nightgown and plush house slippers. Her clothes seem to be an extension of her regal bearing. Moses ushers me over to our host. Lorna gently smiles and leads me out of the room. We venture down a long, dark hallway illuminated by rows of flickering candles.

"How are you feeling?" Lorna inquires.

Although my physical body is in a state of discomfort, I am still floating in the possibility of carrying Obatala's child. "Fine," I say, keeping my thoughts secret.

We enter a spacious room with dark wood floors and very few decorations. There is a large ceramic tub in the middle of the room. Steam floats up from the water. Lorna places the towel on an ornately carved wooden chair. She begins to undress me.

"I've brought you a new set of clothes. You are about my size," she says as she unties my dress and slips it off my shoulders. My senses are heightened, and although her tender touch sends shivers throughout my body, I wish my mother were with me instead. I close my eyes as she continues to undress me. I feel her gently remove my medicine pouch. She peels my bloodstained undergarments from my skin and leads me to the tub. The water is scented with lavender and a hint of salt. I slowly lower myself into the heated water.

"Is it too hot?" Lorna inquires.

My eyes roll to the back of my head in deep pleasure. "It's perfect."

Lorna walks to the windowsill and brings over a bar of soap. Tillie used soap on me when I bathed at her house, but we washed with buckets outside. This ceramic tub is simply delightful. Lorna wets a small cloth and lathers the soap. She reaches over and begins to wash my back.

"Moses tells me this is your first menstruation."

"Yes," I say, completely relaxed under the spell of her nurturing touch.

"Welcome to womanhood. Your cycle is the most beautiful gift of being a woman. We women are blessed with a natural bodily rhythm that keeps us in line with nature. We have our cycles in the very same way that the Earth does. Our moons also wax and wane, powerfully drawing forth our internal waters. Your first moon is incredible medicine. We will bury it in the rich soil after you bathe. It will bless us for the gift."

Lorna washes my entire body clean and gives me a pale blue dress with tiny pink flowers on it. The fresh undergarments are shielded from my blood by a rag. Lorna has shown me how to attach it to a special belt I'm now wearing around my waist under my clothes. She hands me my medicine pouch, and I hang it around my neck. I feel renewed and regenerated. She gives me three extra rags.

"When you change the rag, wash it out, hang it in the sun, and put another one on. It will all become a familiar routine soon."

"How long does it last?"

"Anywhere from four to seven days. It will also come every month now, just as the moon does," she says as she grabs a brush and fixes my hair.

Every month! I try to conceal my dread and disappointment. I don't think that I am made to handle this every month.

"It gets easier."

We head back to the secret room. My walk is awkward as I try to fix the bulky rag. Despite my discomfort, there are so many words of gratitude that I want to share with Lorna, but I can only muster a "Thank you" before my head hits the pillow and I fall asleep.

Through the fog of my slumber, I hear Tillie

repeating my name. I blink my eyes open to see her worried face. "Yemaya, there is word that my uncle is on his way to my parents' house in Cicero. I have to leave now to get there before he does. I must warn them."

"I'm going with you," I say as I jump dizzily from the bed. I lean on Tillie for support.

"Minty thinks you need rest."

"Bring me water," I command.

Tillie finds the water pitcher and pours a glass. She brings it to me. I guzzle it down, grab my leather pouch, and declare, "I'm with you."

Tillie smiles. We rush over to Moses and inform her of our plans. Although she is doubtful, Moses does not attempt to change our minds.

"Never speak of the roads you traveled nor the people who helped you, unless you are leading your own group to freedom," Moses stresses. "We must keep the railroad sacred and secret. The Lord has told me the way and has also told me with whom to share it."

"I will not say a word," Tillie promises.

"Where is your aunt?" Moses inquires.

"She will stay with you. She wishes to go to Canada, where she'll be safe from her husband. He'll kill her if he finds her."

Moses nods and turns to me. She takes both my hands in hers and says, "Remember my vision— New York will not be as you hope. I know your mind is made up, but just be sure that Tillie

230

gets home safely, and then leave immediately for Canada."

"I will," I promise sincerely, squeezing her hands.

She pulls me in for an embrace. I feel safe in her arms.

Moses whispers in my ear, "Remember the roads, for you and Obatala might lead your own group to freedom."

19

CICERO

We travel for days with Tillie in the lead, reading her burnished silver compass. Lorna gave us plenty of food and water to sustain us for the remainder of our journey, and Moses mapped out the course and told us where to find refuge during the days. We travel from nightfall to dawn, becoming one with our nocturnal surroundings.

Tillie unfolds the map that Moses sketched for us. She squints in the dark as she tries to make out our next stop. I look over her shoulder and say, "Nyack. Mrs. Cynthia Hesdra in Nyack."

Tillie furrows her brow and asks, "How in God's good name did you read that?" I smile at Tillie, knowing that I don't really have to explain. Tillie scratches her head and says, "Didn't the sign back there say Nyack?"

"I didn't see it."

We hear a horse and carriage approaching in the distance. Tillie grabs my hand and jumps into the nearby brush. The carriage passes by without suspicion.

Tillie whispers, "I bet they're headed to town.

Cynthia's property is not far from the town square. My parents took me there when I was a child."

She tugs me from the bushes and starts to run after the carriage. The horse is trotting slower than we thought, so we follow stealthily from the side of the road. Under her breath Tillie says, "You are going to love Cynthia. She used to be a slave."

Tillie dodges some trees, then looks back at me again. "Was it her husband, or was it her father? I'm not sure, but one of them bought her freedom, and now she is the richest Negro alive!"

The horses neigh in front of us, and the carriage suddenly stops. Tillie's eyes widen as she motions for my silence. We try to go deeper into the bushes, but the underbrush is too loud to walk on. We slowly crouch to the ground while a large man emerges from the carriage.

"Hello?" he calls out to the trees.

My heart is almost pounding out of my chest. The man pulls a lantern from the carriage and begins to flicker it the same way the Quakers did. He stands quietly as Tillie and I stumble out of the forest.

"Quickly, get in," he says, ushering us into an open carriage as he climbs in the front to drive. "You all fancy yourselves quiet?"

His ginger beard reminds me of the pirates, but that is where the resemblance ends. He is hefty enough that the carriage tips slightly on his side as we start down the road.

He turns around for a moment and holds the light up to my face and whispers, "Dear God in heaven. The whole country is looking for you. Good thing I have more money than I can count, or else I might be tempted to turn you in."

I think he is waiting for us to laugh, but we are silent. He lets out a boisterous howl, then yells, "It's all in jest!" He clears his throat and says, "I'm Theodore Hamilton. I run most of the docks around these parts. I know who you both are; you've been in the paper for the last few weeks."

"The signal you did with the lantern . . . how did you know?" Tillie asks.

"I'm a part of the Underground. Rumor has it that you were traveling with Moses."

Tillie responds, "Yes, she told us to go to Cynthia Hesdra's place."

He chuckles and says, "Cynthia is the only person in Nyack more successful than me. I know where she lives. I'll take you there."

We are quiet for most of the ride, until Theodore breaks the silence. "Why do they call you a witch?"

"I . . . I . . . don't know."

Tillie says, "People will say anything to get their property back."

"That's true," Theodore says as he looks me up and down.

Tillie sees that I'm uncomfortable, so she changes the subject. "I hope Cynthia has some food. I'm starving."

We turn onto a long driveway. Tillie looks around and questions, "Where are we?"

"Cynthia's place," Theodore answers.

"Wait, did she move?" Tillie looks at me and shakes her head.

"Now don't you try anything stupid," Theodore commands.

The horses stop, and he jumps from the driver's bench and grabs us both by our arms. Theodore drags us down the carriage stairs and leads us into a dark barn.

"Now, you listen good," Theodore threatens. "Cynthia has enough money to pay your bounty a hundred times over. If she is supposed to guide you, she will pay for you."

"I thought you didn't need the money," Tillie retorts.

Theodore backhands her. She falls to the ground and lets out a whimper. I kneel down and wrap my arms around her.

"Stay put!" Theodore yells as he shuts and locks the door.

Tillie jumps up and starts to scan the barn. She traces her fingers along the walls, looking for a way out. I see an open window in the loft.

"Up here," I whisper as I guide Tillie up the ladder.

There is fresh hay lining the floor of the loft. In the corner are a pillow and sleeping bag. I wonder if this is Theodore's bed. Before I can form a full thought, Tillie is hanging out of the window.

She looks up at me and says, "Come on."

She lets go and falls to the ground. As she rolls in the dirt, I make my way out of the window. It seems a lot higher than I thought. I hold on to the bottom part of the frame and lower myself down.

A voice calls from the distance: "Yemaya, is that you?"

I drop from the window and land on my rump.

"Oh dear!" the voice yells as she runs up to us.

"Mrs. Cynthia!" Tillie exclaims as she hugs her.

"Tillie! What are you ladies doing? Theodore said that he had you in a safe place."

"Theodore is mad! Totally nuts!" Tillie says as she rubs her cheek where he struck her.

"He is not all there," Cynthia admits. "He is the farmhand for the Hamiltons. Sometimes he is more trouble than help. I gave him five dollars to tell me where you were."

I shake my head as I slowly get up and brush the loose hay from my clothes. Cynthia helps me clean off.

"I live not far from here," Cynthia says. "Let's head to the house. I'm sure you are famished."

• • •

Cynthia's house is beautiful from the outside. White wood trim that looks like lace hangs from the roof. I can smell the evergreens that surround her property as we sneak to the back of the house and climb down into the basement.

"There are many free Negroes here in Nyack," Cynthia says, "but your face is plastered everywhere, so it's best to keep you both down here."

Cynthia has two cots ready for us. Our covered dinner plates are placed at the feet of our beds. The aroma draws us to the food.

"Don't be shy," Cynthia says. "Eat up."

I lift the silver covering to find a steaming plate of roasted potatoes, chicken, rice, and broccoli. My mouth waters as I reach for the fork.

"Yemaya, you haven't said two words since you arrived," Cynthia points out.

I attempt to chew the bite of potato I've just stuffed into my mouth. "I'm sorry. Tillie told me a bit about you. I have never heard of a Negro woman making her own money."

Cynthia laughs. "It's always the money people ask about. You know I was born a slave? Even though my father was a free man, I was not able to buy my freedom until I married my husband. I made boatloads of money after that," she says with a chuckle.

I feel for the pouch of coins that my dear Richard gave me. It's still there, under my coat. I can't help but think of Obatala as Cynthia speaks of her husband. My stomach flutters as she continues telling me about her life.

"Yemaya?" Tillie asks. "Are you all right?"

"Yes, yes," I say as I clench my stomach.

Cynthia continues without noticing my reaction. "What is your plan, ladies?"

"We are going to my parents in Cicero."

Cynthia nods and looks up in deep thought. "One of my employees is riding to Syracuse to pick up a shipment of laundry soap. He can take you that far. Would that be a help?"

"That would be a great help! Thank you, Mrs. Cynthia," Tillie exclaims. "I have an uncle who lives in Syracuse. He could take us home from there."

Tillie reaches for my hand and squeezes it. "We are almost there!"

Cynthia's employee takes us to Syracuse early the next morning. We stay covered in the back of the carriage throughout the entire journey. Cynthia gives us pillows and blankets to keep us comfortable. She also packs fruit, bread, and dried meat. Although the trip feels long, anything beats traveling by foot again. We arrive just as night falls. He drops us off at the top of Tillie's uncle's driveway. Tillie and I venture up the long dirt road. Sweat beads from my pores as we hear dogs barking on his property.

"That's just Honey and Mimi, my uncle's dogs. I haven't been here in ages," Tillie declares as she traces her fingers across the bark of one of the great oaks. Farther down the road stands a vivid red barn. There is a horse and carriage parked out front. I squint to confirm my vision: a man with a bright white mustache sits in front of the carriage. He jumps from the platform and rushes down the road.

Tillie runs to meet him, shouting, "Uncle David!" Then she throws her arms around him.

He lifts her up and swings her around as they both laugh.

"I knew that you would make it home! We have been worried sick over here," he says. "Who do you have with you?"

Breathless, Tillie exclaims, "Uncle, this is my good friend Yemaya! Haven't you seen the posters?"

Uncle David stares at me for a moment, then bows and says, "Any friend of Tillie's is a friend of mine. You're both welcome to stay here, where you'll be safe." He turns to Tillie and says, "I'll take you home when you're ready, but let's fill up first." He smiles gently at me and says, "And where are you heading?"

"I'll travel with you and Tillie, to make sure she gets home safely, and then I'll head to Canada."

David leads us to his white country home with cornflower-blue trim. The landscaping is quaint and simple. There are handcrafted signs labeling herbs in a small garden.

"My wife fancies herself a gardener," he says with a chuckle.

We enter his house through the kitchen door. Startled, David's wife almost drops the tea she's pouring. She wipes her hands on her apron and exclaims, "Tillie!"

Tillie shrieks, "Aunt Rose!"

Rose cups Tillie's face in her hands, kisses her forehead, and says, "My sweet girl! I'm so relieved to see you!"

Aunt Rose flaunts a full head of white hair pulled up into a well-manicured bun. She has maintained a healthy figure, although she seems to be a bit older.

Rose pulls Tillie into an embrace and says, "We have been praying for you, my sweet child. Praise the lord."

"Thank you, Aunt Rose."

"My, my. Where are my manners?" Aunt Rose reaches out to shake my hand. "I'm Tillie's aunt Rose."

"Yemaya," I say.

"My, what a beauty. Isn't she a beauty, David? Let's get you girls cleaned up and fill your bellies with some delicious food."

Aunt Rose gives us a bucket of warm water to bathe on the porch. I reminisce about the comfort of Lorna's ceramic tub as I wring a soaked towel over my head. Tillie begins to shiver in the brisk air. She quickly washes up and runs inside. I'm left by myself on the porch. I drink in the power and strength of the water as it splashes over me. I lather the bar of soap and thoroughly scrub every inch of my body. As I finish, I gather our water and throw it into Rose's garden. I snuggle into the robe Aunt Rose provided and walk inside.

"You will catch your death of cold out there," Aunt Rose says. "Come join the others by the fireplace."

She provides us with fresh clothes and brings out warm cider and apple-cinnamon oatmeal. We sit around the fireplace and rekindle our laughter and storytelling. We decide to stay the night to avoid Uncle David having to travel in the dark. While Tillie is anxious to get home, her uncle says that roads are dangerous without light. Tillie and I exchange looks because we know the dangers of traveling at night quite well.

Uncle David wakes us up at the crack of dawn and informs us that the carriage is ready for travel. Aunt Rose gives us a basket of apples for Tillie's parents and a jar of applesauce to share, then says, "Our trees bore bountiful fruit this year. Next time I will make you my famous apple pie."

Tillie and I jump into the back of the covered carriage and draw the curtains. Uncle David waves goodbye to Aunt Rose and heads down the dirt driveway to the main road.

It only takes a few minutes to get to Cicero, but I'm grateful for the ride. What might have been a night's journey had we gone by foot is only about a thirty-minute jaunt.

Tillie points out the window as we pass by a carved wooden sign that reads WELCOME TO CICERO, NEW YORK.

Just down the road, after we see the sign, Uncle David abruptly stops the carriage. "Whoa!" he yells to the horses.

"Why are you stopping?" Tillie asks. She pulls the curtain open and peers out the window. Her other uncle, Phineas, is standing at the mouth of her gate, holding a rifle across his chest.

"Fancy meeting you here," he says to Uncle David in an eerily calm voice.

Tillie shuts the curtain, and, breathing heavily, she clutches her throat.

Uncle David shouts from the carriage, "Good day, Phineas, fancy meeting *you* here. I suggest you move out of the road, so you don't get trampled."

"I suggest you give me my property so I can be on my way," Phineas snarls.

"I don't know what you're talking about."

At that, Phineas strides over to the carriage, clearly intending to pull the door open, so Uncle David leaps down and punches him in the chest.

Tillie and I watch nervously through the curtains. Moses's words echo in my ear: *New York will not be as you hope. . . . Just make sure Tillie gets home safely.*

At that moment I have a revelation. This is not about me. None of it is. My narrow vision of finding Obatala blinded me to the immense danger and sacrifice that so many people have endured for my freedom. Everything that Tillie has done has been to save my life. This is not about me in the least.

I pull out the leather pouch full of Richard's money and hand it to Tillie.

"What are you doing?" Tillie whispers.

"Buy me from him with the money."

Phineas kicks David to the ground and points the rifle at him. I jump from the carriage, and as he notices me, he lowers his weapon.

Tillie jolts from the door holding the bag of gold coins. She yells, "Take this! It's way more than you paid for her."

Phineas shakes his head and snarls, "It's not about the money anymore." He smashes his gun butt into David's head, knocking him out.

Tillie throws her body over Uncle David's chest and shrieks, *"NO!"*

Phineas kicks Tillie away and turns to me. He says in a flat, cold voice, "If you don't come with me now, I'll kill them both right here."

Tillie weeps as Phineas grabs my arm and pulls

me away. I turn toward her and whisper, loudly enough for them both to hear, "Don't worry about me, Tillie. Remember, I'm a witch."

Phineas yanks my arm and drags me down the road to where his carriage is waiting. He opens the door and shoves me in headfirst. Before I can pull myself up, I see three bodies slumped in the back seat. Huge metal devices are buckled on two of the men's faces and long spikes protrude from collars around their necks. The other man has his wrists tied and is leaning against the wall of the carriage.

"Don't you know it's rude to stare?" Phineas says as he kicks me to the opposite bench. He sits beside me and grabs some shackles from underneath the seat. "Don't give me no more trouble, nigger," he says as he locks me to a railing on the side of the carriage. He looks at his other prisoners, tilts his head to the left, and squints.

"I always get my property back. Haven't lost one nigger yet. Except for the ones you stole from me." He stares at me with an icy glare. I hope that means they made it to freedom. Phineas kicks one of the unconscious slaves in his knee.

The man slumps farther down the wall of the carriage and the long spikes around his neck hit the bench.

"Those spikes must be terribly uncomfortable," Phineas mocks. "I brought them down for you, but as fate would have it, I found all of my niggers."

His voice trails away as I look out the window. Tillie must be scared sick. Moses was right. New York would not be as I hoped. I try to reach my hand to my chest in order to feel the letter from Obatala. It's practically burning through my pouch. Every part of me wants to pull it out and read it over and over again, but Phineas would grab it and destroy it without a single thought.

The carriage wheels rattle as we roll over the cobblestone streets of a small town. I hear a young boy yelling, "Extra! Extra!"

The carriage stops and Phineas jumps out. After a few minutes, the door opens, and the carriage dips with Phineas's weight as he pulls himself back up and settles inside.

He looks at me with disgust and barks, "Keep your eyes on the floor!"

"Yes, Master," I say through clenched teeth.

The carriage rocks as it starts rolling back over the cobblestones. Phineas opens the newspaper he bought from the boy. He pulls out a section with my bounty on it and taunts me, "Mighty fine sketch, don't you think?"

He holds up the picture of me with the words WANTED ALIVE: AFRICAN WITCH. He turns the picture back around and admires it as if it were a fine piece of art. I notice a headline on the back: WHITE MAN CONVICTED OF AIDING THE ATTEMPTED ESCAPE OF THREE SLAVES. Before Phineas folds the paper back up, I see Richard's name in bold print. My heart sinks.

It was only a matter of time before they caught him. The men in his county already knew what he was doing. Phineas notices me straining to see the story. He turns the page around and reads it, then looks up at me, grinning with his thin lips, and asks, "Friend of yours?"

I don't react.

"Serves him right." He throws the rest of the paper out the window, and then holds up my poster once again. "This, I will frame."

I look at his feet, careful not to catch his eye again. My stomach twists into a squid knot as I picture Richard in jail. I spent only one night in one of those cages, and I would not wish it on my worst enemy.

The driver pulls into the train station. I saw many tracks on our journey, but we hid every time a train passed. Those monstrous machines are loud and clunky. The train's whistle blows as Phineas unlocks my shackles from the carriage. I grab my ears and fall to the floor.

Phineas and the driver struggle to pull one of the unconscious men from the cart. As they tug at his arms, Phineas slips and cuts himself on one of the spikes.

"Good Lord in heaven!" he yells as he grabs

his arm. "Don't just stare, you nigger witch! Get up and help us!"

Webs begin to form on my hands, wanting to attach to Phineas's wounds. I wipe them off onto my skirt as I jump from the carriage. I see a glimpse of the limp man's neck. Are my eyes deceiving me?

Three scars . . . This can't be!

As I grab his feet, I get a better look. It's Obatala! It's him! In shock, I almost drop his legs. My heart races as fast as a school of dolphins as I attempt to help carry him to the train.

The crowd of people waiting at the station stare as the three of us struggle to get Obatala to the cart that is normally used to carry heavy baggage. There are gasps and whispers, but no one yells or throws trash at us as they did down south. I lower my head so I don't have to deal with the shame of their stares.

Phineas orders his driver to get the other men. When they return, Phineas points to the back of the train and commands, "Put these niggers in the luggage car."

A man in uniform takes Obatala from us and rolls him down the platform. I follow close behind, with the other two men limping after me. The overseer grabs my arm and we follow the uniformed man to the last car. I see people loading farm animals, trunks, and crates in through the heavy sliding door. I step onto the stairs, and the whistle blows again. I attempt to cover my ears, but it's no use. The driver pushes me in, and I fall over a large crate. The two men carry Obatala into the train car and put him on the floor. They take the other Africans to the next luggage cart.

The men in uniform continue to load animals and baggage until the car is full. I find a place in the back corner with a trunk and sit down. I can barely contain myself.

20

DREAM AWAKE

Obatala lies awkwardly on the train floor. His spikes hold his head up, displaying his scars for me to see. I slowly walk up to my love. My throat tightens as I get closer. I have dreamed about this day more times than I can remember.

I gently caress the raised scars on the back of his neck. My throat closes as I try to say his name. I scrape my arm on the rusted spikes jutting from the metal collar around his neck. I'm shaking. I see the lock and try to pull the collar apart. I pull with all my might, but I am weak. Weaker than usual.

I need water.

I crawl away from Obatala and crash through our train car looking for water. A pig squeals as I pass by her cage. I back up and see that she has a large bucket of water near her, inside. Frantically, I search the side of the cage to find the latch. I'm ecstatic to find it unlocked! I open the door and grab the water. The pig runs out and knocks me over. The water splashes on me, and I can feel my strength returning.

I hasten back to Obatala and rip the corroded

collar from his neck. I find the leather buckle to the metal facemask and break it in half. As the mask falls to the floor, Obatala's body collapses.

His face is so swollen that his eyes are sealed shut. Dried blood stains his lips and nose. Before I can think, webs begin to float out of my body and surround him.

I can feel the energy draining from my system as the silken fibers bind us close together. The wounds must be deep. My webs continue to seal his lacerations.

We are flesh to flesh, in a cocoon of my netting. The light outside our pod dims as the layers of the webs continue to thicken.

I weaken with every second that passes. His breath on my cheek is the only sign of life that I can feel from him. My body begins to shut down. I don't want to miss a thing. I try to keep my eyes open. But I am weak. I can feel my eyes rolling to the back of my head.

"Yemaya," a voice whispers.

I hear it, but I can't seem to move.

"Yemaya, my love," he says with his breath still on my cheek, "am I dreaming?"

I blink my eyes open, and there he is. The sun peeking in from the cracks in the train car seems to form a halo around his head. Web strands hang from his perfectly healed body.

"Are we in heaven?" Obatala asks, touching my face.

He catches a tear from my eye and wipes it away. I know he has so many questions, but I don't have it in me to say a word.

I trace his full lips with my fingertips and gently pull him in for a kiss. His hands timidly caress my back, as if he's still uncertain that I'm real.

I laugh in the middle of our kiss.

"My love, it's me," I say. "And we are definitely not in heaven."

"Speak for yourself," he says as he grabs me for another kiss, his hands gripping my shoulders like he'll never let me go. The strength of his muscles has returned. He looks like the fisherman I once knew.

Atop his muscles, the veins of his arms bulge and branch out like a dark tree. I can't help but trace every crevice and mark on his skin. He's been whipped. More than once. The three scars on the back of his neck are no longer his only ones. I want to be angry, but, gently, he puts his finger on my lips, as if to cease my incessant thoughts.

Obatala kisses my eyelids, cheeks, ears . . . neck.

A surge of energy hits me like an enormous wave, and we both dive in together. He rips off my clothes as my body arches in immense pleasure. He caresses the small of my back and pulls me in close to his chest. My body trembles and the ocean inside of me begins to flow out. His strong arms hold me. Our breath becomes one as we seal our love.

I wake up wrapped in a burlap bag ripped into a blanket. Obatala must have created it while I was sleeping, then drawn it over us. As I blink my eyes open, he is already awake, and staring at me.

"Let's run away," I say. "We can break through these walls."

Smiling, Obatala strokes my face. "It is not just about us anymore. I have a responsibility. I have been working with Moses."

I reach into my little leather pouch, pull out his letter, and slowly unfold it.

He gently covers my hand and begins to recite the poem in my ear, from memory:

You love me the way
Water loves the earth . . .

I close my eyes and feel my heart expand as my love speaks.

"Moses had someone write it down for me. So, she *found* you," he says. His smile conveys both pleasure and surprise. "She is a powerful force, that woman. She told me that we would be in each other's arms again . . ." He stops short.

"What?"

"Nothing, my love," he says, and he kisses my forehead.

Did Moses tell him something dreadful? Like she told me? I don't want to taint my moment with worry. I lay my head on Obatala's chest, and I feel his heartbeat on my skin.

The tracks begin to squeal as the train starts to slow down. Obatala looks at me and says, "It's time."

Reluctantly, I peel away from his chest. My heart seems to stay with him. I already feel the void beginning to grow. I stop.

"I don't want to live without you ever again," I say, trying to hold back my tears.

"I am always with you, my love," he says, kissing my lips.

He walks over to the other side of the car to retrieve my clothing. We dress as the train takes its time pulling into the station. I pick up the metal mask and collar. I am sick. Am I to place this over my love's head? There are bloodstains on the metal. I scratch my nail on the dried gore as I look into Obatala's eyes.

"Be strong, my love," he says, guiding my hands to his face.

He closes his eyes as I place the bloody mask over him. I wrap the large spiked collar around his neck, careful not to harm his three precious scars. The lump in my throat has returned, and I can barely breathe as I prepare him for Phineas.

21

FREE

The master needs to make an example of us before the eyes of the other slaves. The overseer ties my wrists around the same stake I saw after Phineas found me at the river during my ceremony. My fears of being burned at the stake are long gone. Obatala stares at me from across the crowd. They tied him to a tree to await his fate.

As I embrace the splintery pole, the smell of cedar wood fills my senses. I look around at the congregating people, and I recognize almost everyone. The children, Godmother, and the pregnant women, who have given birth to their babies since we last saw each other. All of these people had so much faith in me. They are my family. They are the people who honored and celebrated me, who knew who I was before I knew myself.

"Witch!" Phineas yells as he approaches from a distance.

The game feels old. He cracks the whip on the ground as he nears me. He bellows, "I'll teach you never to run again. I will always find you!"

He slashes the leather whip against my back and rips my flesh apart. My body remains calm and relaxed. There's no longer anything to fight against. The master continues to whip me, lacerating my back with multiple blows. My body becomes weak, and I hang from the stake by my injured wrists.

At the sight of my submission, Phineas ceases the beating and turns toward the slaves. He begins to lecture them on disobedience and punishment. The morning dew, still thick in the air, settles on my freshly wounded skin. My webs slowly emerge and begin to wrap around my back.

Whispers fall from the mouths of the slaves during Phineas's tirade.

Phineas demands, "What are you all muttering about?"

The overseer timidly interjects, "Master, you should really see this."

Phineas rushes to me and violently wipes the webs from my back. He drops the whip and trips backward in disbelief as he witnesses my perfectly healed skin.

"There's . . . there's no way. Impossible!" he stammers.

He turns to the overseer and barks, "Pick up the whip!"

"Sir . . ." he begs.

"Pick up the whip and beat her again!"

The overseer backs away from the crowd and mumbles, "I ain't never seen anything like that in my life."

The congregation of slaves begin to chant: "Yemaya . . . Yemaya . . . Yemaya."

I pull my wrists apart, and the tangled twine falls to the ground. Phineas stands with his mouth agape, frozen in bewilderment. I kick the whip to him and saunter over to the chanting slaves.

I smile. I am free! Not a freedom that I have to prove or see, but a freedom that I can feel. The people gather tools and sticks for protection as they follow behind me. I walk up to Obatala and untie the rope from around his wrists.

Obatala grabs me, wrenches me around, and yells, "No!"

He jumps in front of me.

BANG!

Phineas holds a smoking rifle.

Obatala falls into my arms. I can't stop shaking as I try to hold him up. His eyes say it all. I drop to my knees and lay him down on the bloodstained ground. My webs surround his chest, trying relentlessly to evade the inevitable.

Chaos breaks out around me, but everything seems to be miles away. Obatala struggles to catch his breath.

"Yemaya . . . you are the *One,*" he whispers as his body goes limp.

I hold him. I hold him hard. I don't ever want to live without him again. I don't want this to be the end.

FIVE YEARS LATER

The blue of the ocean beckons as I sit on the white sands. I can hear drums playing in the distance. Cuba reminds me so much of home. The leather pouch around my neck has faded. I pull the tattered letter from Obatala out of it.

> You love me the way
> Water loves the earth.
> Soil, seeds,
> Flowers, trees.
> Pouring forth life.
> Raining down love,
> Gathering in sparkling, crystal drops of light.
> You love me the way water loves me.
> I remember once
> The water of your love
> Became something more . . .
> It was a part of all the water there is.
> And I had to look away from you
> Because in that moment,
> I spied the other half of myself.

"*Mamá*," little Obatala calls as he runs into my arms, his eyes as black as the mysterious realms of the ocean. "*Cuéntame la historia de Papá otra vez.*"

ACKNOWLEDGMENTS

They say it takes a village to raise a child—well, it took a village to write this book! I thank all of my friends and family who read and reread my manuscript. To Charlemagne Tha God and Yadi Alba, thank you for listening to your divine inspiration and making this happen! A special thanks to Marisha Scott; Suzanne Potts; Dr. Velma Love; Michael B. Beckwith; Dr. Yaba Blay; Raymond Garcia; Vanessa Standard; Brett Wright; Leah Lakins; Syntyché Francella; Corey Marshall; k. Neycha Herford; Petra E. Lewis; Laura Cherkas; Chelsea Cohen; Lee Thompson Young; Milena Brown; Raaga Rajagopala; Shida Carr; Lisa Sciambra; Libby McGuire; and my awesome editor, Nicholas Ciani, I could not have done this without you. Molly Findlay, thank you for creating the amazing painting of Yemaya for my cover and Kristina Casarez for creating my original cover. To Kesha Lambert, my beautiful cousin, for taking my author photograph. To Daphne Douge, my ride or die! Erica Dumas, we have been through it! Thank you for standing by my side. To Whitney Davis-Houston, Darya Danesh, Kimberly McCullough, Jan Miller, Ali Kominsky, Nena Madonia Oshman, and Karen

Kinney, thank you for putting those boxing gloves on for me! So great to know I have you all in my corner.

To Mom, you are my inspiration. Dad, you are my motivator. Sharon Kopacz, thank you for believing in me and supporting my process when I couldn't afford to put food on the table. Yvonna Kopacz, thank you for letting me read you parts of the book everyday for years (tears). Michelle and Jove, thanks for keeping me on point, and Michi, thank you for always diving into our imaginations as kids. Nikki, thank you for always believing in me and knowing when to pray for me. Dani and Jatiana, I love you. Sheldon, Sadie, Tela, and Mayan, thank you for your infinite patience. I am so glad you all got to witness this process from the beginning. To my village of amazing friends who have seen me set intentions, write tirelessly, and listen to my endless ideas: Shaman Durek, Doro, Dinan, Sheila, Emmet, Iesha, Jamillah, Cora, Coriann, Natalie, Sabrina, Lee, Javier, Hague, Allison, Ayoka, Nidia, Rachel, Tasha, Adamme, Cathleen, Bonnie, Khairah, Crystal, Domino, Leora, Margie, Malaak, Misty, Onesta, Marzi, Leonie, Bianca, Alyssa, Courtney, Erica, Sarah, Shelly, Tischen, Jason, Jayson, Michelle, Laika, Celine, Chez, Krista, Boris, Nicole, Yona, Sharon L, Audra, Cynthia, Rebecca, Elliott, Daphne, Anel, Chris, Julianna, Angela, Angelique, Joe, Daniella, John, Amaris, Vanessa, Dominique,

Shauna, Jodi, Kehinde, Tai, Danielle, Melissa, Olivia, Nickie, Lysee, Sharmilla, Lisa, Ash, Tracy, Mrs. Ashlock, Mrs. Stallings, Kristy, Anthony, Chuck, Whitney, Mr. Baldwin Style, Courtney, DJ John Quick, Pree, Faith, Alexis, Belyne, Connie, Elena, Kristi, T (Coco Wrangler), Sade, Jamie, Greg, Tiffany, Kim, Elizabeth, Danielle, Lynnette, D'Vita, Mr. Murray, Ina, Jaela,Jasmine, Jenn, Jo-Na, The Julies, Christine, Deb, Erica, Alyssa, Ysabel, Yetta, Kristina, Kyndra, LaToia, Laura, Laurence, Leeza, Linda, Luna, Maritza, Martha, Matt, Meilan, Mariposa, Mercedes, Sari, Taunglea, Tommieka, Tisa, Wendy, ElleVictoria, Christian, Esi, Emelia, Eurila, Faith, Ghebilet, Davena, Don, June, Kasey, Tracie, Stephanie, Ginny, Corwin, Psalm, Chaka, Emily, Norisol, Kyle, Gavin, Bodhi, Camalah, Donte, Kim, Stevie, Aaliyah, Vinnie, Erica, Brianna, Donna, Vida, Nealand, Aiyisha, Venessa, Jacque, Lizzie, Keithley, Yolanda, Jamali, Flo Flo, Pearline, Iris, Debbie, Trever, Spencer, Igal, Juliette, Tanesha, Patty, Richard, Yvette, Stuart, Stanford, John, Eddie, Sonjay, Estherly, Terrence, Grenville, Irvin, Susan, Michelle, Keithroy, Glen, Amanda, Edwin, Sankofa, Doxa, Andreas, Uncle Jurek, Uncle Brother, Auntie Rita, Uncle Keith, Auntie Margaret, Uncle Allan, Aunt Gloria, Uncle Hiram, Aunt Tita, Uncle Eddie, Charlotte, Aunt Cito, Auntie Apple, Uncle Baldwin, Auntie Val, Auntie Brenda, Aunt Chi Chi, Ron, Mary, Ambar,

Jada, Ryan, Vito, Maya, Riley, Jameson, Ora, Chantelle ×2, Collette, Leah, Briana, Jamie, Simone, Lauren, Jade, Jessica, Hanna, Auntie Soph, Uncle Eddie, and all of the rest of my family! To Nana Dot and Pop Pop, thank you for creating my love. All my nieces and nephews, I love you more than words can say: Aiden, Lola, Marley, Sasha, Davis, Xander, Xochi, Althea, Ali, Eden, and Deja.

Last, but definitely not least, I thank God, Yemaya, Oshun, Oya, Idemili, and my ancestors, especially my grandmothers.

ABOUT THE AUTHOR

Anita Kopacz is an award-winning writer and spiritual psychologist. She is the former editor in chief of *Heart & Soul* magazine and managing editor of *BeautyCents* magazine. When she is not writing, you can find her on the dance floor or traveling the world with her children. Anita lives in New York with her family.

Center Point Large Print
600 Brooks Road / PO Box 1
Thorndike, ME 04986-0001 USA

(207) 568-3717

US & Canada:
1 800 929-9108
www.centerpointlargeprint.com